SHATTERED

SOMER GREY

COPYRIGHT AND LICENSE INFORMATION

DISCLAIMER

CONTENTS

SHATTERED

Somer Grey

Shattered

One decision bought a lifetime of debt…

DEDICATION

To dreams and the angels who help make them come true.

ACKNOWLEDGMENTS

My family, who never complained when I spent hours and hours on my computer listening to characters tell me their story instead of time with them. They never grumbled when they were served sandwiches for dinner or asked to wait until I finished my thought. I love you all. Thank you for always supporting and encouraging me.

Aleatha Romig, you're my inspiration. I can't thank you enough for all the advice, support, and encouragement you have given me over the years. Shattered would still be a dream if it weren't for you. Thank you for your friendship and love—you believed in me when I didn't believe in myself. I love and appreciate you more than words.

Tia Louise, thank you for always being there for advice —book, personal, or someone to whom I can vent. I value our friendship and all the laughs we have shared along the way. Thank you for the encouragement and love. Love you.

Kathi Updike, I don't even know where to start. You have been there from the start to encourage and support me. You suffered through first drafts, rewrites, and rewrites of the rewrites all the way up to the end and never complained. Thank you for everything—the help, our walks, and all the talks. I appreciate everything. Thank you.

Gail McHugh, thank you for your belief in me. Always, remember—I believe in you too. Sweets, it's time we take that ride on that kick-ass train.

J.A. Johnston, thank you for all your encouragement and help along the way. Your advice and friendship meant a lot.

Victoria Klick, for all the help and encouragement. Thank you.

A special thank-you to everyone who made this book possible.

My cover designer, Judi Perkins, for my beautiful cover. You took a simple idea and brought it to life.

My editor, Lisa Aurello, you took a rough gem and turned it into a perfect sparkling diamond.

I also would like to thank all the people who encouraged me in the early stages of this story. I appreciate it.

PROLOGUE

MELISSA

Every action has an equal and opposite reaction, at least that was what they told me in physics. Decisions made had the potential to change, manipulate, and mold a person's life. Women believed it was their prerogative to change their mind and in solidarity, other women honored that privilege. Most decisions were based on our experiences and upbringing. The past typically ruled and dictated decisions and continued to influence them far into the future.

Although an individual should have every right to select her path, not everyone was afforded that right. Sometimes other people created obstacles or hurdles designed to detour the chosen path for their own ends. In my case, circumstances set into motion by others wouldn't be revealed until it was too late to change the consequences. The cards that were dealt had to be played—win or lose. It wasn't over until the last card was drawn. Just as in the game of blackjack, a gambler had no control over the cards. The only choice was to fold or stay and take a chance.

Life was about choices—forks in the road. One way directed you to happiness and the other to tragedy. At eighteen, cunning decisions had left me two options: a life of betrayal and deception or fidelity and truth. Both held promises for more but also came with undesirable consequences. Neither of the opportunities would reveal my entrapment into the unknown until the decision was made.

I stood at a theoretical fork before me and considered which road would pave the way for the best chance at my future. One path led to financial freedom while the other was filled with economic struggles. I chose to follow the one that appeared to be the easier: one year of employment with Infidelity in exchange for my dream of attending the school of my choice. Although going that route might have seemed to be the easiest financially, physically, and emotionally, the price would turn out to be much steeper than I anticipated.

It was never exclusively my decision—unbeknownst to me. My future would be influenced by a man who manipulated and changed the course of my life. Obstacles were placed in my path to ensure that his fantasy of taming a redheaded firecracker was fulfilled, guaranteeing that the road I picked intertwined my dreams with his desires in ways I wouldn't understand until it was too late.

Looking back, my childhood dream influenced so many of my decisions and left my life in the balance of others. I wasn't more than a fly to be swatted away when I became a liability to the future of Infidelity, a company that catered to the wealthy and entitled. I lost the right to decide for myself—all of my future decisions made have been determined by those with their own best interests and agenda. I was insignificant—a means to an end to ensure that the power stayed with the powerful.

I finally admitted to myself that the agreement that funded my dream opened the door into the world ruled by wealth and power. The consequences dispensed were determined by the person who paid the most money. I wasn't the princess from a Disney movie who found her Prince Charming. A knight in shining armor wouldn't swoop to my rescue. My happily-ever-after wasn't written in the stars. The story of my decisions wasn't a fairy tale—it was a nightmare that crushed my dream and left me shattered.

CHAPTER 1

Plan Set into Motion
Two years earlier

Peyton

I concealed her picture between business and credit cards in my wallet. It was my daily treat to help pass the time until she was mine, not that I needed the image to fantasize about her. Every detail of her being was burned into my memory. The first time I saw her was last month at a surprise birthday party my wife insisted I attend. I owned Harrison Imports, a multibillion-dollar company, and her insistence wasn't something I often entertained, but I was tired of hearing her bullshit, so I went. My secretary was instructed to call an hour into the party to inform me of my excuse—a company emergency in Chicago. My private plane was fueled and ready for takeoff the moment

I left the party. Company emergencies or contract issues were my go-to excuses to free me from my home.

I wasn't a good husband, and my wife wasn't 'June fucking Cleaver' from *Leave it to Beaver*. I cheated on her, and she knew it. Hell, she walked in the night before our wedding to find me with my dick in some other woman's mouth. Our marriage was one of convenience. She conveniently spent my money, and I conveniently used her for information she was privy to from her employer, information that grew my company and my finances into the fortune it is today. It was the perfect arrangement until her biological clock began to ring. Now, she wanted us to have a real marriage and kids. That shit wouldn't happen. I had no interest in children and decided on a vasectomy long before we ever met. I just omitted that information before our arrangement began. At the time, I believed it was a need-to-know status quo. *I* needed to know. She didn't. I refused to be tied to some bitch for the rest of my life when she 'accidentally' missed her birth control.

I pulled my beautiful girl's picture out of my wallet every day since I stole it from my wife. Shit, the only reason I hid it was because of who she was—forbidden fruit. I knew it was wrong, but she consumed my thoughts. I imagined all the dirty things I would do to her as I worked my morning wood in the shower. It was my only relief from blue balls. My dick didn't even jump anymore with my wife's touch—I had to pretend it was my sweetness.

The minute I walked into that party, all I saw was the most beautiful face framed with long red curls. This sweet beauty was at least six inches shorter than me, had a tiny waist and plump breasts. Her vibrant green eyes bore into me as my eyes ran up and down her sexy body. My gaze stopped at the prettiest red lips, meant to be wrapped around my cock as I face-fucked her. When she ran her tongue over her desirable lips, my dick twitched.

My dick ached, begging for release from the sweet beauty headed my way as my wife introduced me to her friends. We may have been married for years, but this was one of the few times I ever interacted with these people. I nodded attentively and never heard a word. It was a skill I'd perfected over the years. I was a master at manipulation with the ability to maintain an impression of interest even when there wasn't one. I'd conducted video and conference calls while my dick was being sucked without so much as a hitch in the conversation.

When my beauty reached us, the rest of the world faded away. All I saw was her sexy-as-sin eyes and pale skin meant to be marked by me. I imagined her bent over my bed and her bare ass high in the air for me to take. In my fantasy, she would plead and beg for me to fuck her, but I'd refuse until my belt left her ass as red as the hair on top of her head. My grip would tighten around her already-bruised hips as I pumped in and out of her. As the scenes played in my mind, my dick raged to be touched by the feisty firecracker in front of me. My thoughts were filled with all the possible things I could do to her. I pictured her on her knees, hands tied behind her back, as her greedy mouth devoured my cock to the root.

Fuck. I needed to calm down before I took her and

fucked her in front of all these people. I hadn't had a reaction like that to a woman since I was in college.

My wife's touch brought me back to the party and the conversation at hand. "Darling, this is Melissa." I had no idea what she said prior. "Melissa, this is my husband."

"It's nice to meet you, sir."

Her radiant smile, sweet voice, and the way she said "sir" made my dick almost shoot its load. This beautiful creature had me mesmerized—until one little gesture sent a knife to my heart: someone called for cake and placed a crown on her head for all to sing *Happy Birthday—sixteenth* birthday.

Physically, I appeared unfazed, but emotionally, I was rocked. I'd just imagined fucking a sixteen-year-old girl. Admittedly, I liked them young, but fuck me if I would cross that legal line. Usually young and perky meant twenty or twenty-one. I knew there was no way I could wait another four or five years to sink my dick into her. It was going to be torture enough to wait the two years for her to turn eighteen, but I refused to touch her until she was of legal age.

I left the party and tried to forget her, but those lips and eyes haunted me. I dreamed of her, jerked off to her image, and even fucked my wife with Melissa's face in my head. Hell, it was immoral, but that only fueled my desire. No matter what I tried, I wasn't able to forget her. That was when I decided that I needed a plan to ensure that she would be mine once she was eighteen. I knew I wouldn't stop fantasizing about her until I had fucked and licked every damn inch of that body. My lust for her was insatiable, and I hadn't even touched her yet.

A year later, plans were set in motion with just one phone call. Phase one was initiated when she turned seventeen years old. With that call, I controlled every aspect of her future, and it didn't matter to me that she wasn't eighteen yet. She would soon be my puppet, and I would be her puppeteer. The string that once held her dream now was cut and reattached to my control. I would own her and her future, no matter the cost. I gave no fucks if it was wrong. I wanted the feisty redhead with bright green eyes, and I wouldn't take no for an answer.

One more swipe of the mouse and the money was transferred offshore before being transferred back to complete payment. My money allowed me the liberties others couldn't afford. This transaction secured a spot for my beauty. Soon, her dream would be achieved, but only if she followed my trail of breadcrumbs. The deal was sealed. My soul was signed to the devil. I would probably spend eternity in hell, and it cost me a fortune. But fuck, I knew no matter the cost, having my redheaded beauty would be worth it.

Now came the next step.

∼

One year after the 16th birthday party

BLOCKED CALLER: *"It's done. I expect payment by the end of the day."*
Male Voice: *"Dead?"*

Blocked Caller: *"No, as you instructed—injured."*
Male Voice: *"Good, payment delivered per your instruction."*

~

Several months after the call

I ROCKED the oversize office chair back and forth as I hung up the burner phone I used when I didn't want things traced back to me. I had just implemented the final phase to ensure that Melissa's destiny was set and that it would be the one I planned. A year from now, Melissa would have the chance of a lifetime. If she wanted to attend her dream college, she needed to accept the option that would be presented to her. In a year, we would both have our dreams. She would have the admission to a top university, and I would have her in my bed.

I thought about my wife's request for me to employ sweet Melissa. Her appeal worked out perfectly for me. However, I feigned annoyance. I knew she would nag until I hired the girl. If I'd been too eager, my wife would have questioned my motives. The way it played out, I was now able to watch and control Melissa's future from my office, and no one was the wiser. Per my request, human resources placed Melissa in the mailroom. The placement would help to quell any office rumors of nepotism. It wasn't that I cared what people thought—this was my damn company—but I found out early on that sometimes the hands-off approach worked best. In reality, I had my hands very much on—their bodies.

As a mail separator, Melissa would never actually step foot in my office. That didn't stop the images of me fucking her that I conjured up in my mind. Each time I closed my eyes, my fantasy of Melissa continued and played out in my imagination.

Leaning back, I imagined that a blinking red light on her office phone would inform her that I needed her in my office. She would softly knock before she entered.

"Yes, sir?"

"I understand you were late."

"I'm sorry. I woke up late and..."

"I accept no excuses, Melissa." My voice would be harsh. *"I cannot tolerate tardiness."*

"But sir, I—"

Of course, I wouldn't allow her to finish—this was my fantasy. I've dreamed of this scene since I was a teenager and walked in on my father fucking his secretary. Initially, my fantasies didn't include Melissa. But since I saw her at that damn party, she was the only one I saw when my eyes closed.

"Melissa, come closer. I don't like to yell across the room, especially to my assistant."

When she entered, she was my PA, but by the time she reached my desk, she would be my personal fuck toy. Even in my imagination, Melissa knew how to drive me crazy with her wild red hair pinned back in a bun, a loose strand framing her face. She approached my desk swirling a ball-point pen in her mouth. Each step exposed more of her long legs under her short skirt. A low-cut blouse revealed the top of her breasts, and her dark nipples teased me as they showed through her white blouse. My mouth watered, and my dick hardened as my fantasy played out in my head.

The pen rested against her lips and then slid back into her mouth deep. She pulled it out as she approached, licking her red lips. Her tongue darted in and out as she chewed on the tip of the pen. Her walk slowed before she reached my desk.

"Sir."

Oh, the way she said the word sir made my dick even harder, and she knew it. Another step closer and she dropped to her knees before me. Her small hands rubbed the outside of my black designer pants. Slowly, she unzipped my trousers, reached into my boxers, and wrapped her tiny fingers around my stiff dick. Her touch sent a shock wave up and down my spine. She squeezed and rubbed the silky skin until it stretched into a hard rod against my stomach. She blinked a few times, lowered her head, and licked the pre-cum off the tip just before she devoured my cock. She sucked and pulled with the perfect pressure along my length.

Melissa looked up at me with those sinful eyes; my dick popped out of her mouth, leaving a beautiful red ring from her lipstick on my shaft. I would never be satisfied with just her mouth on my dick—my cock needed her warm pussy.

"Strip now!" My tone was harsh and demanding.

"Yes, sir. Did I do something wrong?" Her sweet innocent voice echoed through.

"Tardiness deserves a reprimand. Sucking my cock is a privilege, not a penalty. Your ass will take your punishment. Now, strip and lay across my lap. Five strikes with my hand should be enough to remind you not to be late—next time I'll use my belt." As she obeyed, her naked body lying over my lap, I rubbed her beautiful ass, dipping my finger lower into the desired spot that my dick begged to be in, balls deep.

"I want you to count; this is only the first part of your punishment." I'd positioned my dick, so when she lay across my lap for her spanking, she'd rub against me. Each strike left a raised red handprint on her perfect ass and pushed her pussy downward, allowing my dick to kiss her mound and drive her crazy. Skin-to-skin but not enough pressure to relieve her.

"Five."

"Now, get up and sit on my dick—I believe my dick wants to punish your pussy—or maybe I should fuck your ass."

Without hesitation, she took what I gave. *"Yes, sir."*

Fuck, I needed relief from this fantasy. My dick ached to be touched, but the receptionist who frequently filled my needs was out of the office. I was too hard to leave my office in search of someone to help relieve my hard-on. If I wanted to get any work done, I needed to pull myself out of my pants and jack off. My hand replaced Melissa's heavenly body. One stroke and another, it wasn't the same as a warm pussy, but it had to do. My hand continued to pull when my phone rang, bringing me back to the present.

Ignoring the call, I let it go to voicemail as I worked my dick faster. My mind focused on Melissa's body, I pulled my cock even more fiercely. A few more yanks and I groaned in relief as I came harder than I had in a long time. Even so, I still had a semi.

After a few minutes of panting, I walked to my private bathroom to clean myself up. One more year until my fantasy and Melissa's dream became a reality. I just hoped I could last that long.

CHAPTER 2

The Pain

Melissa

Tick. *Tick. Tick.* The noises from the hallway were drowned out as the large wooden door closed. The cold air sent a chill across my heated skin. The collision of the two temperatures confused my body. One minute it was on fire, and the next, chills ran down my spine. Neither would be victorious in their battle to overtake the other. Their fight would end in a draw as a thick layer of sweat coated the goose bumps.

It didn't take long, but eventually, I became numb to the temperature sealed into the room—it had evaporated into the fog that captured my mind. I felt absolutely nothing anymore. Everything was distanced as my mind blocked the commotion inside of the room. Its only mission was to find a safe place to hide, a spot where no one would discover me. Physically they would be able to see me, but mentally I would be lost to the world. I searched the room until the clock in the center of the wall came into focus. I hoped it would protect me and help me find the peace needed to escape. My eyes locked on the clock's face, and I waited to be welcomed. Voices and noises finally vanished beyond my reach; I was no longer part of the world of hurt and betrayal. My mind created a new place—one of love, comfort, and above all, safety. Dark black arms welcomed me into its world and held me close. In reality, the rest of the world saw only a clock, but to me, it was the fortress that protected me from the truth. The inanimate object allowed me to escape, blocking me from the stares of sympathy and judgment. The thin hands stretched across the white face and slowly ticked, yet as the minute hand moved to the next number, nothing changed—time stood still. One minute wasn't any different from the one before, even though the hands sat on varied numbers. I didn't care because for now the clocked welcomed me into its king-dom, giving me a small piece of salvation. Soon, the only thing I heard or saw was the ticking of the clock and the hands on the face.

Tick. Tick. Tick.

Real-time continued outside of my cocoon, but my new world embraced me and kept all the memories and pain of the last hours in the shadows. Everything disappeared into the bright light. I submerged myself in the darkness, or maybe I had gone into the light, and the world stayed in the dark. I wasn't sure anymore. Memories of my child-hood flashed before me.

It was a time when life was much more straightforward.

My only worries were the color of the dress to wear or who I played with that day. I stopped and smelled the flowers on my walk to school and sometimes brought scissors to cut one. I remembered once when I was caught cutting a purple rose from our neighbor's garden. Suddenly, it was all gone. I cried out, but no one listened. "Wait, don't go."

A firm hand squeezed my shoulder bringing me back again to the here and now. The clock and memory were gone, and I was back in the cold, sterile room I'd escaped from earlier. The bright light shone down, and all the sounds from before bore into me. I didn't want to return to this horrid place. Why did they insist upon my return?

A soft-spoken woman attempted to talk to me—her words were thoughtful and careful not to alarm me. She viewed me as the trapped animal cornered in the room with no escape.

"Melissa, I am Dr. Caller." She knelt in front of the wheelchair where I sat and waited for my eyes to reach hers before she continued. A small smile and her soft blue eyes told me to trust, but my judgment had misled me in the past and wasn't something I had faith in at the moment. Dr. Caller brought her hands to my knee to earn my confidence. Her fingers were thick, and her face had soft lines around her eyes and mouth.

"I'm going to be the one who examines you. Can you tell me what happened?"

Her voice was gentle, and typically it would soothe me, and her tenderness would comfort, but this room refused to allow me relief. The bright lights and disinfectant smells took the luxury of peace away. My eyes darted around the

17

room. She may be the one who would examine me, but we were not alone. The room was filled with others—so many eyes upon me. The judgment I'd felt moments ago multiplied. Now, not only was there a doctor and the man who found me, but two female nurses, a male police officer in a blue uniform, and another man whom I assumed was a detective since he was dressed in a brown suit.

"Sir, we need you to leave."

I wasn't sure who said it, but I panicked and grabbed the hand of the man who found me. My fingers dug into his skin like he was the only thing that kept me afloat. My words were lost, but my eyes told the story of my fears as they darted around the room before they again landed on the doctor with blond hair. The message was clear: I didn't want to be left alone with strangers—even if they wanted to help me. Terror traveled throughout my body, tremors shaking me uncontrollably. I needed someone familiar even if that someone was the man who manipulated me into a life of lies and deceit. No matter the past, now he was my only lifeline.

The doctor leaned toward me and gently placed her hand on the side of my face, bringing my attention back to her. "Melissa, do you want him to stay?"

My fingers wrapped even tighter around his hand as I pulled it closer to my chest and nodded.

"Okay, he can stay—but he'll need to leave for a few minutes while we collect your clothes. He will be right outside the door." She nodded to the door with a half window covered with a curtain.

I held his hand a few more minutes before I released it. Once he and the ugly-suit man left, one of the nurses helped me stand and led me to a screen to disrobe. A white sheet lay below my feet with several boxes filled with supplies lying next to it as the nurses stood off to the side.

"Melissa, my name is Julia—one of the nurses who'll help you. I promise no one will hurt you." Her voice, like the doctors, was soft and patient, but it didn't calm me. She was about the same age as the doctor, but it appeared that time had been kinder to her.

Our eyes met—hers a dark blue and mine probably a glassy, dull green. I listened to the nurse's instructions as I clutched the plush beige blanket wrapped about my body.

"I need you to take off your clothes, one at a time, and place them in separate bags, which I'll hand you. I'll label each bag, seal it, and initial it to preserve the evidence for the police."

I nodded, still unable to speak. Looking at her and then the ground where the sheet lay, it was as if she read my mind and answered.

"Anything that falls from your clothes will land on the sheet. That will also be placed in a bag to ensure evidence isn't lost."

I didn't want to shed the little protection I had. It was my last shield before all the shame of what had happened was revealed. I dropped the blanket in the first bag already labeled. The nurse carefully picked up the bag, folded the top, and affixed tape that was marked evidence before she initialed it and handed it to someone on the other side of the screen. She must have sensed my anxiety because she stopped to explain that it was the officer on the outside who would place everything in a box labeled with my name.

I felt more naked than ever before. The blanket had been my only defense, and now it was gone. I spent the next ten minutes like a robot—an assembly line of pain and hurt slowly removed. The blue sundress was the next piece of clothing to follow—I hadn't noticed the top and sides had been ripped in the struggle for freedom from my attacker. Next, my bra; it too was broken at the strap, my breasts no longer supported. The final piece was my panties—they hung from my hips, but the crotch had been ripped open. Once I handed her my tattered panties, she gave me a gown to slide over my bare body. It may have covered my most private parts, but it didn't cover my indignity.

The second nurse walked over. "I need you to lie on the table. The doctor will examine you, and take oral, vaginal, and anal samples for the rape kit. She will also exam all your cuts and bruises. Dr. Caller will dictate her findings to a recorder to ensure nothing is omitted from her report. The officer will also be taking notes of anything he observes. After your exam, we will need to photograph your injuries."

The second nurse continued. Her voice grated on my nerves as she delivered the protocol rape-procedure speech with no emotion. I didn't know if she was a cold, heartless bitch to everyone or if she saved it for me for some reason. I just knew I didn't want her as a nurse, but didn't have the strength to argue.

The scowl on the first nurse's face when she approached us told me that she didn't like nurse number two either. I wondered if the tension had more to do with the dislike of each other than me, but at that moment, I didn't give a fuck.

A few minutes later, ugly-suit man and my savior walked back into the room—neither looked happy, but again I didn't care.

"Detective March will take your statement for the report. Melissa..." The second nurse continued.

The last thing I heard was Melissa. I didn't listen to any more of her words; they disappeared into space. I didn't care. I just wanted the next part of my journey into humiliation to end. But it had only begun as my legs were placed in the stirrups and my knees spread. I wondered which was more humiliating and degrading, being raped or having every inch of my body poked, prodded, and photographed. My heart knew that the doctor and nurses were trying to help me, but it didn't stop the shame. I needed out but I wasn't sure out of what—out of the room, the hospital, or just my mind.

The doctor quietly spoke as she dictated her findings, "....bruising on both left and right upper thighs. I need pictures of this area along with..."

I closed my eyes as my legs were pulled farther apart, and a cold metal instrument entered my body. I felt the pressure build and the pain from the insertion. I also felt the dishonor. Everything the doctor saw was announced into a recorder, and every swab and sample were inserted into labeled bags and then sealed with tape and initials. The uniformed officer then placed each one in the box that contained the bags of my clothes. The box now was a representative of my life—secrets and pain sealed away for others to discover.

CHAPTER 3

My Shame

Melissa

Memories of what brought me to the hospital and the sterile room filled my mind. I didn't want to remember. I needed to forget, to stop the movie on continued replay in my mind.

I refused to take part in what was happening; I needed my clock—the one that held me and kept me safe. I forced my eyes open and searched for my salvation, the thing that allowed me to bury the pain. Soft ticks came alive, and the room disappeared once again. The sounds of the clicks grew louder and louder until they became a calming heart-beat lulling me and providing my refuge. The clock's hand surrounded, embraced, and welcomed me from the reality of what my life became—they provided freedom and happiness. My eyes closed as the newfound peace took over, and the clock completely accepted me back.

Peaceful thoughts flooded my mind. I was in a garden filled with flowers and trails. The sounds of feet hitting soft sands filled the salty air as the view of the single path split in two with a large wooden sign centered between the paths. "Choose wisely" was scrolled across the top, and below were two arrows. One pointed toward the right and the other the left, but nothing was written under them. I walked closer to the sign and noticed a message in tiny print at the very bottom: "One road leads to peace and happiness and the other to pain and suffering." There was nothing more. It didn't say which path led where. I walked toward the right, where flowers adorned the paths—beautiful colorful roses bloomed. As I continued down the right side of the road, the bright sun shone. There were blue skies and singing birds. I walked in awe of the beauty when suddenly, a brisk wind blew, kicking up sand as massive black clouds rolled in and covered the path in a thick fog.

Within seconds, the light of the sun disappeared, and darkness surrounded me, leaving me in the murky haze. The sweet scent of the roses turned sour, leaving a strong odor of decay—the beautiful blossoms were no longer vibrant, but all dead—the stems bent over and the petals brown and lifeless.

My journey to the right side of the fork changed from peaceful and happy to dreary and sad. More winds whirled through, dirt tornados spun, and debris rustled through the air. Another gust raged, yet the leaves eerily stilled as the wind whispered its words.

"Once you have chosen, you can't turn back."

A sharp pain pulled me back from the trance I'd insulated myself with to avoid the hurt. The distant voices became louder.

Now, both worlds—my imagination and my reality—were hell, both filled with dread. I didn't want either, but then again, no one asked me what I wanted.

"Bruising to the vaginal area..."

I didn't want to know—I needed to drown out all the voices, especially the one that insisted on revealing my disgrace in vivid details. More specifics of my abuse were described, but a male voice dominated over the softly spoken one.

"Melissa, sweetheart, can you hear me?"

I knew that voice. It belonged to the man who introduced me to a new way of life—a life that an eighteen-year-old never knew existed. He'd shown me more in the first few months of our arrangement than I'd seen in a lifetime. He had been gentle and understanding with me, teaching me what he expected. Even the times when I hadn't followed all of his guidelines, he'd showered me with gifts and kindness. He'd promised punishments yet laced them with rewards.

I fell in love with the man who held my hand—not with the man he became in the last few months. In the beginning, he spent hours with me... until he didn't. I longed for the early days of our relationship. That was the escape I longed to relive.

Now, my disgrace would have no rewards, only punishments and heartbreak. I committed the one unforgivable crime and broke the cardinal rule of our contract. In our time together, he only required and demanded one thing—my fidelity to only him.

This man owned me—my body, mind, and soul—from the minute I agreed and signed my life to him. His protection was supposed to ensure my safety. Once he learned the truth, I'd lose that security. I'd often had that reminder repeated to me: he would not protect me if I disobeyed—I would be on my own. His empire and image came before his dirty little secret—me. Though he may have truly cared for and adored me, I had no doubts: to save himself he would discard me like yesterday's trash. Now, all the lies I'd hidden and everything I'd worked for during the last six months, everything to accomplish my dreams, was all for nothing.

Another squeeze brought me back to the room of hell— the voices, smells, and pain all returned. One tear had multiplied into many until my eyes drowned in the hot liquid and overflowed into a trail down my face. My mind fired question after question, but actual words became lost before they surfaced. I already knew the answers to the questions; it had been my desires and my decisions that had brought me to my now. It was my fault—even if others tried to convince me otherwise. I'd signed the agreement, and I'd broken it by not following the rules.

Last night's attack wouldn't be the only consequence I paid.

I wanted—no needed—out of the horrid nightmare I was living. My feet were still secured in stirrups and legs bent as I lay on the small mattress covered with a white sheet. A second white sheet was on top of me, but its place-ment left my lower half exposed to all in the room.

I was nothing more than a rag doll to the robot nurse. She'd placed the sheet over my arms at my sides and proceeded to pull the rat's nest of my hair through a small comb into little envelopes. Her motions were rough and uncaring. With everyone else's eyes diverted, she didn't seem to care if she caused me pain.

The nicer of the nurses approached with a bottle and needle and inserted medicine into the IV. "This is going to help with the pain."

Dr. Caller gently took my legs out of the stirrups and covered them with the sheet. She walked to the head of the bed and reached for my hand. Our eyes met as she described each abuse my body had endured. She continued her observation in more detail than I wanted as I stared at her with blank eyes.

"Melissa, you sustained a lot of trauma. There are bruises in your vagina and anus. Your right arm is sprained, and several of your ribs are bruised. You also have multiple lacerations—including your lip, which is split. I gave you an antibiotic. It will help with any infections. I'm also prescribing..."

Once again, someone else was making the decision of what they thought they knew I needed. No one needed to tell me my injuries—I'd lived it. I didn't want to relive the details again.

I just wanted to disappear.

I couldn't listen anymore. All the pain in the world wouldn't compare to the pain I felt in my heart. The rape was more than a physical attack. The marks on my skin served as a reminder of a night of terror. It was the hidden scars locked into my memory that would haunt me. I was no longer the Melissa Summers with a dream but now Melissa Summers, the violated rape victim—shattered beyond repair.

As hard as I tried to drown her out, Dr. Caller pulled

me back with her words. I overheard the conversation she had with the nurse. She wanted me admitted for observation for the night and possibly the next. Dr. Caller had more concerns about my mental state than my physical injuries. She knew my body would heal but emotionally, she worried I would have difficulties since I still hadn't uttered a word since being brought to the ER.

The words echoed off the walls as the fog that surrounded me lifted. I didn't care about the why and what they were doing—I just wanted the voices to stop. I needed the room, people, and bright white light gone.

I searched again until I found my clock and begged for its warm embrace. The gracious clock forbade entrance to anyone else—this was *my* safe place. The words of pain and punishment were banished outside the welcomed heartbeat. The ticks lulled me into peace and took me somewhere else.

CHAPTER 4

Broken Dreams
Eight Months Prior

Melissa

L ife was full of decisions and opportunities but also loss and disappointment. When I was about ten years old, my parents and I went to Chicago on vacation. We visited all the usual tourist activities. One of the attractions in a neighboring city included a trip to Northwestern University. Immediately, it captivated my heart. The world-renowned history and culture came to life, and I begged for more information. I fell in love and dreamed of becoming a student there, a place recognized for greatness both internationally and nationally. So many great scholars had walked along the paths at Northwestern, and I wanted to follow those same tracks to my future. My determination to attend Northwestern kept me focused and ensured I would find a way to live my dream.

I spent the next seven years studying, achieving high grades with the hopes of a scholarship to offset some of the expenses. From the time I entered high school, weekends were spent prepping and reviewing for the SAT. The only time I set my academics aside was when I was at work. I didn't have time to socialize. Admittance to Northwestern was more critical than interaction in my mind. I didn't realize how much I lost until I didn't have many friendships left. Life went on without me in my quest for success.

At the beginning of my senior year, I filled out the application to Northwestern. A section of the application asked why I wanted to attend this university and what were my future goals. I completed the form, listing all the reasons why Northwestern was my first choice of higher education. I explained that I wished to be part of the history associated with Northwestern, that I had since I was ten years old. I believed that it was the place where I would be able to receive an excellent education; after all, it was one of the top business schools in the nation.

At seventeen, I didn't understand how quickly life could change, virtually in the blink of an eye. I was naïve with the mindset that nothing bad would ever happen to me. I received a rude awakening a few weeks after my birthday when my father was involved in a car accident. Someone ran his car off the road and into a shallow ditch. The other driver didn't stop and never was found. That person just left my father in a mangled car until an anonymous caller reported the accident. By the time the fire department rescued him, he'd been trapped in his car for over an hour.

His recovery was slow, leaving him unable to work, and without his paycheck, my parents struggled financially. They were forced to use the money they'd put aside for my college fund for everyday expenses. No matter how much my parents wanted to help me with college costs, that one accident made it financially impossible.

Nevertheless, my dream stayed intact, even if I had to work harder than expected to reach my dream to attend Northwestern. The obstacles only made me more determined.

Though my father's accident and parents' financial struggle left so much of my future uncertain, I believed I'd earned a place in my dream school. Days before my graduation I received the letter from Northwestern about my scholarship application. My hands shook as I ripped open the envelope and read the words that changed my life forever.

DEAR MISS SUMMERS,

Thank you for your application submission to Northwestern University. We're honored you chose our school as one of your college options. However, we regret to inform you that your application for a full-paid scholarship was not approved. We are confident with your high GPA and SAT score that another college will be able to accept and accommodate your financial needs. We urge you to reapply in the spring semester as new grants and scholarships open yearly.

DEVASTATED WOULDN'T HAVE BEEN close to the correct term I would use to describe my reaction. I stared at the letter, but the words blurred. A single teardrop fell on the paper, smudging the ink. I should have expected it. I should have sent other applications back in December when I called about the status of my application. It was still under review —they were waiting for final approval and funding for several grants.

The letter dropped to the floor as I ran to my room and locked the door. I needed time to process the rejection. I'd worked so hard to achieve my dream—valedictorian and 1590 on my SATs. I knew other students had gotten into their choice college with lower scores, but maybe they hadn't requested a full ride. The wind was knocked out of me. Northwestern didn't want me. As painful as that was to admit, it didn't change the fact that I still wanted to be a part of Northwestern.

I walked through the next few days in a haze. Nothing interested me anymore, including the address to my class-mates that I was required to give at graduation. The speech I had prepared no longer held relevance to me. I felt like a kite lost in the wind with no string to guide me. I wanted to kick and scream at the top of my lungs, proclaiming that it wasn't fair. All the time I'd spent in school and work and the lost friendships were all for nothing. If I learned anything in the last year, it was that life wasn't always fair.

I pushed through the heartache even though I didn't want to sit on that stage. I refused to let anyone know my shortcomings, my failures. Lost and emotionally drained, I stood at the podium and gave my speech. I spoke of dreams and opportunities, made empty promises that if my fellow students worked hard enough, dreams would come true. My address ended with the hope that one day we would all see our dreams fulfilled. I stood with confidence in my words, my eyes hiding the pain, my heart bleeding with every lie that came out of my mouth. I forbade my failure to be identified by anyone. Everyone assumed that I would attend Northwestern. In the event that someone would ask for confirmation, I would smile and assure them that everything was in place. They didn't need to know the truth. They hadn't earned the right to my pain—no one had. I just couldn't say that Northwestern had rejected me. I wouldn't. It was still my dream.

My mother's best friend had set up a little graduation dinner for me before we learned of my rejection from Northwestern. I didn't feel festive. What was there to celebrate over graduating high school? In my mind, that wasn't a huge accomplishment. My mother liked to say that the university hadn't rejected me; they'd declined a full scholarship. She could wrap all the pretty paper around the truth that she wanted to, but it was still bullshit. Whether they excluded, refused, or rejected my entrance to their university, it boiled down to one thing: I wasn't good enough.

I argued with my mother most of the day to cancel the dinner. I had maintained and hidden my disappointment, showing fake happiness through my graduation. They were people I didn't care about, but my mother's friend was different. She'd been like an aunt to me. I wasn't sure I would be able to fake enjoyment with people I cared about.

"Melissa, I know you're disappointed, but this could be a good thing. You can attend college closer to home.

Besides, Regina already made the reservation, and you always loved your time with Regina."

"Mom, I don't want to go."

"Darling, Regina said Peyton would be there, and she said she would talk to him about a possible job at his company. It would look bad if you didn't show up. The job won't be anything fancy, but it will undoubtedly pay more than you make now."

"So this isn't a celebration—it's a job interview?" I snarled back. "And why is Peyton going to be there? I've met him, like, once or twice."

"I don't know why he's coming. Regina asked him to come so they could spend more time together. According to her, they've been trying to work on their marriage."

"Great, so it's a job interview, marriage-building session, and celebration dinner."

The sarcasm didn't make my mother happy. My mother was beautiful with bright green eyes and dark brown hair cut short in the back and longer in the front.

"That's enough. I've had about enough of your mouth, Melissa. You're smart. You can still apply to another college for the fall semester, one closer to home… maybe even take online classes at first and reapply to Northwestern for spring. Maybe more grants will be available."

"Sure, Mom, Northwestern wasn't something I dreamed about since I was, like what, ten." The hurt was evident in my voice—or maybe it was pure anger. Deep down I was angry at everyone and everything. I was upset with the person who'd hit my father and caused the financial hardship, at my parents for not planning better for my college, at Northwestern for not accepting me, and more than any of those, I was mad at myself for not working harder. I'd failed, and it cost me my dream.

"Stop! It was a dream. Now face reality, Melissa."

"Mom."

"Don't want to hear it. Get your butt in the shower so that we aren't late. Regina wanted to do something special for you—don't ruin her night, too."

"Whatever. I'll go, but don't expect me to pass this job interview." I knew it was rude, but at the moment I didn't give a fuck.

"Watch it, get yourself changed, and while you are at it, adjust that attitude. Stop feeling sorry for yourself."

What the hell did she expect from me—to be happy? Northwestern had been my dream, and now it was gone. Why didn't she understand? It wasn't just disappointment I felt but like a piece of me had died. Since receiving the rejection letter, I'd spent hours every day lamenting my worth. The confidence to succeed in college was no longer a certainty. What if I wasn't smart enough?

That letter was not only my downfall, but would become the path that led to a series of decisions never to be reversed.

Regina had made a reservation at a little restaurant in Myrtle Beach. Before we left, I threw one more spoiled-brat tantrum, begged and pleaded not to have to go. It didn't work, and there we were, about to walk into the restaurant thirty minutes late. The look my mom gave my dad after she texted Regina made me even more nervous. I'd only met Regina's husband a few times, but I'd overheard stories. From all accounts, he was a dick, one who didn't tolerate anything—especially tardiness.

Peyton and Regina were seated at a table that over-looked the ocean. As we approached, my mother whis-pered, "Peyton doesn't look happy."

My mother was right. His expression frightened me. And then I felt worse because as scary as Peyton looked, Regina looked even more terrified. Peyton stood up as we approached. He shook my father's hand as my mother and I hugged Regina. My father pulled the chair out for my mother while Peyton pulled the empty chair next to him out for me.

Peyton continued to stand until I sat and pushed my chair beneath the table. He said something under his breath that I swore sounded like "this shit won't happen much longer."

"I'm sorry we are late..." my mother continued.

Peyton looked around the table, smiled, and interjected. "Please, don't mention it again. Let's just enjoy a night with friends."

Regina and my mother stared at each other in shock at his response. I heard the last time someone was late, he'd reprimanded them for wasting his valuable time. Friend or not, he didn't care. Peyton was a successful businessman, and he had high expectations for himself and everyone around him. He didn't tolerate rules broken without penal-ties, and I was positive that punctuality was one thing he demanded.

Peyton turned toward me as the words passed his lips, and our eyes met. He appeared relaxed. The arch of his brow lifted, and his eyes bore into me as if he could read my every thought. I wasn't sure if it was nerves or the way he gazed at me, but my stomach clenched. His expression gave me chills. Strangely, I wasn't sure if the way he looked at me scared or excited me. What the fuck—why was I even thinking thoughts like this? He was married to my mother's oldest and best friend.

Regina was my mom's age, but she looked more like a trophy wife. Her blond hair was perfectly styled with large waves that hung over her shoulders. Regina's makeup always looked like she'd just walked out of a magazine photo shoot.

Peyton was a little older than my parents and Regina, yet he looked handsomer than men half his age. When he'd stood to help me with my chair, I noticed that he was at least six inches taller than me, and I was wearing three-inch heels. He was lean but muscular; his black designer suit fit perfectly. One could wonder what it hid. His black hair was peppered with a little gray, and he wore a five o'clock shadow, which was also highlighted with gray. He had a square jaw, high cheekbones, and dark brown eyes that commanded attention. Peyton was sexy as hell, and his presence—for some unknown reason—brought a sense of peace to me.

Laughter and conversation filled the table. Peyton commented and joined the conversation a few times, but he mostly listened and watched. I observed him too. For some reason, he intrigued me. To anyone who viewed our table from the outside, he appeared as involved in the discussion as his wife and my parents, but that wasn't the reality. His boredom was evident to me while the rest of the world saw an animated persona.

Once the conversation turned to my college plans, I was done. For the first time in over a week, I actually felt something again. And the mere mention of Northwestern took me right back to where I had been before dinner. The sad story of my rejection filled the table. I refused to listen anymore. I already knew this chapter in my life and didn't need to reread it. The charade was over, and so was the night. I wasn't sure if I cried for the anger or the hurt. I pushed my chair back and left the table. I needed fresh air. My parents would text me when they were ready to go. Until then, I wanted to be alone.

The sky had darkened, and the temperature cooled since we'd entered the restaurant. I walked along the shore with the sand between my toes until I found the perfect spot to sit. My feet hung in the shallow water that surrounded a large rock. It was hard and uncomfortable, but it was peaceful. I lost time listening to the waves crashing the shore and watching the moonlight shining down on the dark water. I'd visited this beach a hundred times, but I'd never taken the time to really take in all the sounds and smells. It was refreshing and freeing. It could be so easy to lose myself in such a peaceful place. I closed my eyes and let the wind temporarily take all my pain away.

CHAPTER 5

Opportunities

Melissa

A few days after I sat on the beach, I realized I needed to stop feeling sorry for myself. I listened to my heart and opened it to new possibilities. I still wanted to attend Northwestern, but that wouldn't happen this semester. I needed a path to living my dream. I decided to take the fall term off from college courses and work as much as possible to build my savings. I might not be able to get a fully paid scholarship, but there were opportunities for grants, students loans, and partial scholarships. I was willing to chance one semester off in return for a longtime dream. In the event that the spring term brought rejection, then I'd concede that it wasn't meant to be, and I needed a change of direction for my future.

Regina came through with a job offer from Peyton's

company, Harrison Imports. I was hired to work in the mailroom. She made sure to tell me I wouldn't receive any special treatment. In fact, I probably would have to work harder than anyone else since she'd pressured Peyton to find an opening. I didn't expect a free ride or special treatment. I just needed a foot in the door to prove I was capable.

I delivered the mail to the lower offices at Harrison Imports, and someone else was responsible for the upper floors, which housed the executives. The job was boring and tedious but paid well, and the hours allowed me to babysit at night. A few weeks before my eighteenth birthday, my life hit another bump. The knock sent me on another emotional ride that rocked my self-esteem. I'd lied to myself if I believed I'd overcome the rejection of Northwestern—I'd just buried the pain.

All the hurt and self-doubt crashed back when I ran into a former classmate, Meagan, at a local restaurant. She and several of her friends sat a few tables over. At one time we had been close, but that all changed when Northwestern became my only focus. She waved across the tables, and I did my best to pretend not to see her. Meagan was determined. She walked over to our table, with a fake smile plastered across her face. I had the feeling she'd picked the short straw, which left her responsible for getting the scoop on the fallen valedictorian.

"Melissa," she said.

"Hello, Meagan."

"I'm surprised to see you here in Myrtle Beach during the fall semester. When are you going back? You must be so happy that you were accepted."

I smiled at her.

"I remember that Northwestern was the only college you wanted to go to when we were in school. Maybe we can get together when I'm up there next week?"

"Yeah, um, I decided to take the fall term off," I lied. "I needed a little break and wanted to spend some time with my mom." I knew that she knew, and anyone she told would know that everything I said was a big fat lie.

"Oh, w-well," she stammered. "I need to get back to my friends. I just wanted to say hello. It was good to see you." She passed our table and headed back to her group of friends.

"Mom, can we go?"

My mother saw the pain in my eyes and nodded to the waitress to bring the bill. I heard the snickers and remarks as we walked by them. "OMG, she didn't get in."

The laughs I heard cut me deeply, and a shadow of a doubt would linger within me, influencing future decisions. That's when I realized the agony of the rejection letter wasn't gone, just buried. I'd sugarcoated my failure with hope, which was only another failure on my part because I'd actually believed that lie... until I didn't.

The short visit with Meagan showed me how cruel and callous people could be. After that, I withdrew from the outside world. The only time I left the house was to go to work. Harrison Imports kept me occupied during the day. It was the nights that were longer with the lack of sleep I maintained. The little bit I did sleep was thanks to an old-fashioned alarm clock that still ticked away the minutes. Just as some counted sheep, the clock's ticks were my salvation, lulling me into sleep.

I'd learned that life wasn't fair, and since I'd run into Meagan, life became even more mundane and boring. From eight to five, I delivered mail to offices, and the rest of my time I spent in my room alone. Every day was the same until I received a text on my way to my car after work.

UNKNOWN NUMBER: **Happy 18th birthday. Wishes do come true.**
Me: Who is this?

WHEN NO ONE RESPONDED, I figured it was the wrong number. My birthday had been a week ago; the message should include 'belated' if it were for me. Placing my phone in the cupholder, I noticed an envelope on my passenger seat. Confused, I looked around my car to see if anything was missing. The letter was the only thing out of place, and I knew my car doors had been locked when I left. My instinct to secure the door kicked in, but that was stupid. If someone got in once, that person could get in again. I looked around the garage but didn't see anyone; even the other coworkers who'd left when I did were now gone.

First, the text and now some strange envelope placed neatly on my car's seat. I stared at it like it was a snake ready to strike. It took me five minutes to get the courage to pick it up. Once I did, I flipped it back and forth. It was thick linen paper with my name scrolled across the front in black ink, written in old calligraphy font. The back was sealed with red wax with an engraved "I" impression. Ten minutes of inspection and I still hadn't opened it. I wasn't sure why I was afraid. Finally, I slid my index finger under the wax, popped the seal, and found a second envelope devoid of writing. Inside the second envelope was a folded letter. Carefully, I pulled it out, feeling that if I moved too fast it would explode on impact.

DEAR MISS SUMMERS,

You have been chosen along with several other candidates for a second opportunity to attend Northwestern University. I work for a company that helps young students achieve academic success by matching future employers with potential employees. All of our clients provide financial support that includes a fully paid scholarship and room and board to students who have shown great promise toward the future.

One of our benefactors has become aware of your circumstances and would like to give you the opportunity to complete your studies and achieve the education of a lifetime. We respect the privacy of our benefactors, as well as possible clients and employees. Therefore, we will not divulge the name of the company nor the benefactor unless you're chosen as the recipient of the scholarship.

To be considered, we require an extensive interview that will take place in New York. All of your travel expenses will be paid, along with financial compensation for your time if you agree to meet with one of our agents. Please know that not all applicants will be chosen; however, based upon our research, you appear to be a viable candidate for this program.

Our company prides itself on the successful matching of future client and employee. Please contact me, Karen, at 646-XXX-XXXX immediately. We look forward to hearing from you.

Best,

Karen Flores

WHAT THE FUCK WAS THIS?

I sat in my car and burned the letter into my memory. This shit had to be a joke, but why would someone fuck with me? The better question was who?

I crumpled the paper and threw the letter on my floorboard. And then I began to reconsider. What if wasn't a joke? What if Northwestern was in my future?

I needed to find out if this was real. If it wasn't, someone went to a lot of trouble to fuck with me. I uncrumpled and stretched the paper three more times before I dared to call the number.

Once I found the nerve to call, I dialed and hung up a few times. By the time I finally called and connected with the person on the other end of the call, my heart was pounding and my hands shaking. I had so many questions I wanted to ask. "Why, who, and how did this company know about me?"

I was certain that this entire setup had to be a prank, but I wasn't about to take the chance that it wasn't. The letter, if real, could be the only solution, the only way for me to attend Northwestern. In the small amount of time

I'd been working, it was obvious that I would never be able to save enough money for a university like Northwestern. Whatever this was, it could be my last opportunity to fulfill my dream. One way or the other, Northwestern's doors would either be opened for me or slammed in my face. I couldn't not call. I needed to find out what my future held.

CHAPTER 6

New Experiences

Melissa

Despite my unease, after the call, I decided to travel to New York and interview for a chance at my dream. The trip occurred about a week after I found the invitation on my car seat.

I saw it as an opportunity I couldn't pass up. One interview could give me a chance. Beyond that, by accepting the invitation, I received an all-paid vacation and five thousand dollars cash. I didn't have anything to lose, provided it was legit and not a scam to kidnap and sell me as a sex slave. My instinct was that the interview was real, but my gut also told me there was a hell of a lot more to this meeting.

Who paid someone for an interview and covered all that person's expenses to find a future employee?

Unexpected obstacles had inundated me over the last two years, and I had two more to climb over to get to New York—my parents. With all the complications, one thing never strayed too far away and that was my determination. Even though I had weak moments and wanted to give up at times, my resolution pushed me further.

Karen promised to handle the hurdle of my parents. It was one of the things we had talked about during the initial call. The itinerary she sent included a forged invitation to attend a college open house in New York. It was supposedly a seminar to help college students apply to top US schools and increase their probability of being accepted. I didn't know if anything like that existed, but neither did my parents. As dangerous as it was to lie and give my parents bogus plans, I took the risk for my dream, for Northwestern. There was also the bonus of a trip to New York with all expenses paid.

Monday afternoon I boarded a nonstop flight to New York. Karen had everything arranged from the moment I stepped onto the plane until I reached the hotel. Once I arrived, all I needed to do was text the number she provided, and a car would pick me up. The flight landed at about five thirty. I sent the text to the number in the email.

ME: I just landed.

WITHIN SECONDS my phone dinged with a message for me to proceed straight to the pickup and drop-off area of the airport. My luggage was sent directly to the hotel for my convenience. I walked out the automatic doors into the bright sun and the smell of exhaust from the traffic of cars that lined the curb.

A man in his mid-twenties approached me and lowered his hat. He nodded and gave a professional smile. "Miss Summers?"

"Yes, I'm Melissa Summers."

"My name is James. Karen Flores sent me to pick you up and drive you to the hotel. If you're ready?"

He didn't just open the back door to a white stretch limo—he opened the door to a whole new world.

I nodded. "Thank you."

I wasn't sure how James managed to arrive in a matter of minutes, but I had a feeling this was the norm for Karen's clients. I leaned down into the back of the limo. Shock wouldn't even come close to my reaction. I was overwhelmed.

My reflection on the screen reminded me of a kid in a candy store with wide glossy eyes. Excitement like I'd never felt filled me. I had imagined my arrival in New York a hundred times, and never did a limo enter into the fantasy of the illusion. At that moment, I realized that no matter what happened in that interview, my life would change forever. Outside of the vehicle, it was the everyday world, but inside it was like I just entered the Twilight Zone of the rich and famous. Only a small minority lived in this world, and Karen had invited me into the sandbox to play.

The limo was new. I closed my eyes and inhaled the scent. Expensive. There was one thing I knew for sure: this car wasn't a rent-by-the-hour limo. It was owned and operated by a wealthy individual or by a company who served only elite clients. As I sat on the cool black bench seat that faced the front, I ran my hands over the seat. The leather was creamy and felt smoother than that in standard cars. Installed between the two individual seats behind the driver was a fully stocked bar with high-end liquor and variously sized crystal glasses. The privacy divider wasn't a typical screen that raised and lowered but a large monitor hooked to a laptop and secured to the top of the bar. The air conditioner kept the back of the limo cool even with the slider open to the sunroof as the sun shone through the glass top.

The limo became silent as James shut the door; the outside world disappeared. The car horns, echoes of voices, and the loudspeakers vanished. James opened the driver's door, and only the slightest bit of sound reentered. The screen didn't prevent all noise from entering, but it buffered most of it. The inside of the limo was like a sealed vacuum from the outside world, keeping it private. A small laugh bubbled out of me at the thought of a soundproof limo.

"Miss Summers," James said as he handed me a heavy linen envelope. "Ms. Flores wanted you to open this before we arrive at the hotel. It has everything you need for your check-in."

"Thank you." I hadn't even noticed the divider down until he called my name. Honestly, I wouldn't have noticed much because I was too busy taking in my surroundings.

As I accepted the envelope, he turned and the privacy monitor rose. The envelope was the same as the one I found in my car a week earlier, consisting of thick linen paper. This one too had a blob of red wax imprinted with an "I" at the edge of the lip. I slid my nail under the seal to open it. I pulled out a stack of twenties with a note attached to the first bill.

MELISSA,

Please use this cash to tip the doormen and bellhops at the hotel. James is one of our employees and does not require a tip. Your hotel confirmation number is 5984546. Instructions, dining cards, additional cash for tipping, and all the information needed for your visit will be sent to your hotel room once you arrive. Please read and follow the directive as it is essential for your interview.

Karen Flores

THE LIMO SWERVED through the New York traffic for thirty-plus minutes as I watched the city pass by through the window. We passed areas with massive steel and glass towers interspersed with older buildings with historic character. No matter where we drove, the streets were littered with everyday people. The limo slowed, and James pulled toward the curb and stopped. The silence vanished when an older gentleman opened my door, and the noise of the city came back in stereo. A dark hand reached in to help me out of the backseat. I looked up and stopped.

"Welcome to the Ritz Carlton Hotel. It's an honor to have you here," greeted the gentlemen who opened my limo door. He was dressed in a long black coat and a top hat that matched that of the second man who held the hotel door open for guests as they entered.

All the words I wanted to say to describe the beauty before me were lost somewhere in my thoughts. I'm not sure when James approached from the other side, but he handed me my purse and the envelope I left on the seat.

"Miss Summers."

I turned toward James.

"All of your luggage has already been sent to your room. Please call Karen or let the hotel know if you need anything. It was a pleasure to meet you. Enjoy your visit." He bowed his head before he turned away and walked back toward the driver's seat.

"Madam," the man who opened my door said. "Billy will escort you to the reservation desk and to your room once you're checked in." He gestured toward a younger man dressed in livery.

I placed a twenty-dollar bill in his hand. I wasn't sure if that was too much, but I figured if Karen expected me to give less of a tip, she would have included smaller denominations. "Thank you."

The doorman and Billy probably thought those were the only two words in my vocabulary. It was just so surreal, and I wasn't able to keep up with the pace. The older gentleman opened one of the double doors and gestured for me and Billy to enter. I went first with Billy a few steps behind me.

Every few minutes poor Billy would misstep when I stopped with no warning. The hotel was absolutely beautiful, and I just wanted to soak it all in. Glamorous was the only word that came to my mind to describe it. The floors were cream-colored marble or tile—I wasn't sure, but it exhibited such elegance. The reservation and concierge desks were a warm oak finish, each stylish and welcoming. Once my feet started to move again, we passed the concierge and headed to the reservation desk.

"Good evening. May I help you?" the person at the desk asked as I walked by.

"No, thank you. I just need to check in."

"Welcome to the Ritz Carlton. I'm Samuel. If you need anything, please let me know. I'm here to make sure your stay is everything you imagined."

I smiled at him. "Thank you." I had become a broken record with *thank you* on repeat. The only positive was that I managed to give Samuel an actual answer. Billy walked with me to the reservation desk and waited as I registered.

"Hello, may I help you?" a young blond receptionist asked as she smiled. She didn't appear much older than I was.

"Yes, I'm Melissa Summers, and I have a reservation."

"I just need your reservation number and identification please."

I handed her the confirmation number from the envelope that James had given me and my driver's license.

"Yes, Miss Summers, we've been expecting you. Your room is ready, and your luggage was sent up a few minutes ago. I just need you to sign here, and then Billy will show you to your room and make sure everything is to your liking."

"Thank you." I smiled.

"Enjoy your visit. You will find a list of numbers next to the phone. If you need anything at all, please let us know."

Billy and I rode up in the elevator in silence. Once the doors opened, Billy signaled for me to proceed. I followed to the end of the hallway, and he used his master key card to open the door.

"Holy shit!" My jaw dropped. If I'd thought the entrance was dazzling, it paled in comparison to this room.

"Do you need anything else, Miss Summers?"

"Shit." I laughed. "No, thank you."

"Let us know if you need anything."

"Billy, wait." I reached in and pulled out two twenties and handed them to him. Again, I wasn't sure if it was too much, but he'd escorted me from the limo to my room and deserved a larger tip than someone who'd simply opened the door.

When the door to the room closed, I jumped on the bed like a two-year-old child, bouncing with excitement. I jumped one last time and dropped on the large plush bed. As I lay there staring at the ceiling, I thought about everything. It was all so surreal. I'd never expected a first-class flight, limo, and hotel. It was so over the top—a world I could never have imagined.

This hotel was the most beautiful place I had ever visited. There was only one other place that came close— Regina and Peyton's house in Myrtle Beach. My hotel room furniture was all done in a warm oak: the bed, desk, and nightstands were from the same collection. Across from the bed and nightstands was a desk with a TV mounted on the wall. A gold Victorian wingback chair was in the corner with a panoramic window a few feet from the nightstand. The spectacular view overlooked Central Park. Tall trees below were sprinkled with yellow, orange, and brown leaves. The park was surrounded by tall and short buildings. Time stood still as I gazed out onto a river of color outlined with barges of gray steel. A knock on the door woke me from the daydream of possibilities.

I answered the door, and Billy stood there with a large basket in his hands. "Miss Summers, I have a delivery for you."

Once Billy left, I walked to the bathroom. No, it wasn't a bathroom: it was a fucking spa. I mean all hotels had bathrooms, most being small with a basic white tub, sink, and toilet. The bathroom in this hotel wasn't just an ordinary hotel bathroom—it was architectural art. A large garden tub separated the walk-in shower on one side of the room and a brightly lit vanity on the other. Little bottles of soaps, oils, shampoos, and bubble beads rested on the step of the garden tub. Silk flowers sat in modern vases on the granite counter and glass shelves stacked with candles were next to the oversize mirror. A door was off to the side, which led to the toilet hidden in its nook.

When I left Myrtle Beach, I'd hoped to have some time to explore the city. But instead, it seemed that tonight would be spent on the gift basket Billy had delivered. As I ordered room service, I sat on the bed and inspected the basket with a locket shaped tag hanging from the top.

Welcome Melissa, from Karen.

I untied the red bow, pulled out a thick envelope, chocolates, crackers, gourmet coffee, and flavored teas. I opened the chocolate box and snagged a piece and then moved on to the letter within the envelope. Just as on every other correspondence, the back of the envelope was sealed with an "I" embedded in red wax.

MELISSA,

Welcome to New York. As you know, your invitation to interview for this program was based on your stellar academics and the recommendation by one of our bene-factors. We pride ourselves on the successful matching of employee and client. To that end, we have provided you with the resources to ensure your success. Your success is our success. I have scheduled the first part of the interview for Thursday morning. Please follow all the instructions provided in the remaining envelope. I will be in touch with you on Wednesday to finalize the time and transportation for the interview.

Karen

I FLIPPED the top of the envelope. Inside was another note, a few business cards, a prepaid credit card, and more cash. I didn't even want to imagine how much this trip was costing or who paid for it all.

MELISSA,

Appointments have been made on your behalf with each of the boutiques enclosed. Days and times are written on the back of the individual cards. Each shop has a list of the different attire required for your inter-view. Financial arrangements have been prearranged and will be billed to us directly by the boutiques and spa. Included is one thousand dollars prepaid credit for any nonessential items you may need. I have also enclosed additional cash for future tips. Tips are not required or expected at the boutiques. However, please be sure to tip each salon specialist at the spa. Tips for room service or another hotel chargeable should be added to the room.

Karen

HOLY SHIT, I felt like I'd won the fucking lottery—without having to pick the actual numbers. The rest of the night I tossed and turned with little to no sleep, wondering if the entire week would be as overwhelming as today.

Tuesday was occupied with boutiques and shopping. Instead of asking for transportation, I walked, believing it would be the only way I would see New York with all the appointments tightly scheduled.

The first boutique I entered made me think of the scene from *Pretty Woman*. The saleswomen hovered over me just as when Edward took Vivian shopping. They brought crystal glasses of water for me to sip while they showed me outfits waiting for my approval or disapproval.

I tried on each outfit that I liked until three appropriate business garments were selected. The next boutique was for formal wear. It was a repeat of the first store, but along with the water, little sandwiches were provided as a snack. All the stores were instructed to send selected items straight to Karen once I passed the interview part of the process. The final boutique sold lingerie. I spent just as many hours in search of it as I did the other items requested. I must have tried on every color before settling on matching bras and panties in red, black, and white.

Though, I never knew intimate attire was part of a professional interview, I admitted, if only to myself, that wearing it made me feel sexy as hell. The saleslady said that I was to take this purchase with me because I needed to look confident during my interview.

According to the saleslady, confidence came from within. The undergarments provided that. She said that I needed to feel worthy, and the best way to achieve that feeling was to look worthy.

By the end of the day, I was exhausted. Instead of walking, I hailed a cab and made my way back to the hotel. My big plans to explore the city changed to a hot shower and dinner in bed.

Dinner arrived about an hour after I returned to the room. Pulling the serving tray next to the bed, I ate. After dinner, I snuggled into the covers. The next thing I knew, I woke up to the sun shining outside my window.

Wednesday was much the same as Tuesday, but instead of clothes shopping, I was pampered. I spent the entire day in the spa being treated like a princess—haircut, pedicure, manicure, and a full-body massage to help me relax. By the time they finished with me, it was again time for dinner. I debated on the downstairs restaurant, but at the last minute decided again on room service instead.

My phone buzzed just after I opened the door to my room. It was a New York number, but it wasn't the same one Karen had called from before.

"Hello?" I asked as well as answered.

"Miss Summers, this is Karen Flores."

"Ms. Flores."

"Melissa, your interview is set for nine tomorrow morning. I have talked to the boutiques and everything will be delivered to my office, assuming the interview goes as I hope."

"I didn't—"

She cut me off. "James will pick you up at exactly eight-thirty. Melissa, this is a very long process and will take much of the day—don't keep James waiting." Ms. Flores never took a breath as she spoke to me.

I wasn't sure if she always talked like that or if it was to ensure that I didn't have a chance to interrupt her.

"Melissa," she went on. "I know this sounds extensive, but we at our company pride ourselves in making sure that all of our applicants have the best chance of success. If the first benefactor chooses another candidate, your application will remain on file for a potential match to other clients. I'm sure you have questions, but please save it all until tomorrow."

"Thank you, Ms. Flores. Is there anything else I need or should do before tomorrow?"

In a stern voice, she went on. "Melissa, the most important thing is punctuality. Do not be late. It will reflect negatively on your application."

"Karen—" I tried to continue, but she cut me off. Anything else I had to say was lost.

"Tomorrow, Miss Summers." And then the line went dead.

CHAPTER 7

The Interview

Melissa

I woke up Thursday morning, showered, styled my hair, and applied my makeup, but everything after that was a blur. I wasn't sure if I was more excited or scared. I followed the saleslady's advice—*you have to look worthy to feel worthy.* Something told me it should probably be said the other way around. You needed to feel worthy to look worthy. Hell, I didn't know anymore. I just knew I needed to look and act the part, so I found the new sexy and expensive bra and panties and put them on. After I did, I stood in front of the mirror and cried. I literally cried because no matter which way the saying went, I felt it— worthy. For the first time in longer than I could remember, I felt worthy. Yes, I was still nervous, but a sense of calm had magically fallen over me.

I could do this.

I would kick ass in the interview and finally be the girl who got her dream.

Karen had explained during a call that if I was chosen, I'd have specific responsibilities to maintain. At times I would have to attend social functions, and to that end, I needed to demonstrate my ability to appear professional and elegant. It was why the shopping spree was essential and necessary for the second part of the interview. All of the clients of Karen's company enjoyed a high financial standing, and as such, they had an expected image to uphold.

At precisely 8:25 in the morning, I walked out of the hotel and was greeted by the driver who picked me up from the airport. James held open the door to the backseat of a black limo.

"Miss Summers," James said as he approached.

"Yes."

"I'll be driving you to your interview this morning and bringing you back once you are finished."

I smiled and took a deep breath of the New York air that surrounded me—it felt different from home. One could smell the salt in the air in Myrtle Beach while here, the odors of the street filled the air.

"Thank you." I lowered my head and entered the back seat of the limo. It wasn't the same one that picked me up from the airport. Once again, this limo was fully stocked with alcohol. Whoever employed Karen had a shit-ton of money and had no problem spending on luxury. It was more than I ever imagined. I couldn't help but think that even if I didn't receive the scholarship, I experienced more in this trip than I would have in a lifetime.

We drove for about twenty minutes before we pulled up to a tall building made of glass. James opened my door and escorted me into the building. We passed the receptionist and security guard to head to a bank of elevators without even stopping to check in. James pushed the up button and waited until the doors opened, and we both stepped in. I walked toward the back, and he went straight to a control panel and inserted a key under the numbers.

He turned to me. "The elevator is programmed. Once the doors open, someone will greet you and take you to your interview." He turned back around and left without another word.

When the doors opened, I was greeted. "Miss Summers, I'm Hannah, please follow me."

I didn't get a chance to respond before she turned and headed in the direction of a large oak desk with several chairs on the side.

"Please, have a seat. Ms. Flores will be with you in a few minutes."

"Thank you."

I laughed to myself when I thought about Ms. Flores's warning about not being late. Just as with a medical office, tardiness only applied to the person who had been requested, not the one who held the appointment. Apparently, her punctuality was not essential. I pulled my phone out to check my messages and waited.

Someone approached and held out her hand. "Miss Summers, I'm Karen Flores."

I accepted her hand and thanked her for the opportunity to interview for the position.

"Please, come in and have a seat. I'll be in with you in just a minute." She held her door open for me to enter, and her secretary approached and handed her some papers.

Ms. Flores shut the door and walked to her desk. "Melissa, nice to finally meet you."

"Thank you for meeting with me, Ms. Flores."

"Karen, call me Karen." She smiled. "I explained to you on the initial call and the invitation that our company holds a strict confidentiality policy. Anything said or done from this point forward is sensitive. The information you're about to learn may not be divulged to anyone including your family or friends. Therefore, before we begin, you are required to sign a nondisclosure agreement. It is at your discretion, but if you do not wish to sign, your interview will end here. Your expenses will be paid and your account credited the five thousand dollars we agreed upon, but no other discussions will transpire." She handed me the NDA. "Melissa, I know this is a big decision; therefore, I'll have Hannah escort you to a private room to review the paperwork in private. If you agree to sign, we can begin your interview today."

I read the NDA as Karen suggested; the contract was basic. The terminology was above my head; the way lawyers wrote contracts was more complicated than necessary. Honestly, I didn't need to read the contract for the name itself explained it. Nondisclosure agreement. You can't repeat anything you see, hear, or do, outside of those who are privy to the arrangement.

Simple.

After fifteen minutes, I went back to Hannah's desk and handed her the signed NDA. "I'm ready to talk to Karen."

"Have a seat, and she'll be right with you."

I waited for about fifteen minutes before Karen opened her door. "Melissa, please come back into my office."

We both took our seats, Karen behind her desk and me in the leather chair in front of it. She shuffled some papers before she began.

"You understand that from this moment on your NDA is in effect? Anything said is confidential and prohibited from being discussed outside of this office. If you breach the NDA, fines and other legal action can and will be taken against you."

"Yes, ma'am."

"Good, let us get started. I work for a company called Infidelity. We match clients with prospective employees. However, our clients do not hire the employees for their businesses but for companionship. Just as the word implies, you would spend time with the person who holds your agreement. As an employee of one of our clients, you may be required to attend social events. Time alone in private settings would be at their discretion."

Karen took a breath and continued as if she didn't just say *private setting*. I had no response except shock and OMG wrapped up nicely to say WTF. She stopped to gauge my reaction before she began again.

"I'm sure you have a lot of questions, but before you ask, please give me a chance to explain more about the service."

Karen spent over an hour detailing the ins and outs of Infidelity. Wealthy clients paid a monthly allowance, college tuition, and all room and board expenses in return for companionship. Many clients were workaholics and didn't have time to date—they required a companion to accompany them to social events. Others were in relationships and when stressed needed a place to find comfort with no expectations.

Karen never mentioned sex, which said more than if she had. A company wouldn't be able to sell sex legally, but *companionship* wasn't sex. Therefore, there was no law prohibiting it. Infidelity had a loophole within which to operate legally as long as the service provided was strictly companionship. If the client and employer chose to engage in sex—well, it wasn't part of the signed arrangement.

After the interview with Karen, I was sent on to the second part of the interview, a lengthy evaluation with a psychologist. I was also required to have a medical exam to ensure my health. Infidelity needed to confirm my physical and mental health before I could be considered. I answered more questions about myself, sexual experiences, and topics that seemed entirely irrelevant.

All of it took up the entire day. By the time I was done, I had no more energy for anything. As glamorous as this trip was, I wouldn't see much of New York because every night since I arrived ended in exhaustion.

CHAPTER 8

The Agreement

Melissa

That night, I sat in the large hotel bed with the packet Karen had given me. The first document was the nondisclosure agreement I'd signed before the interview began. And behind it was a thick stack of forms I needed to review and complete.

I placed the NDA on the bottom of the stack and proceeded to read the requirements to be an Infidelity employee. I would be required to provide one year of companionship to a client in exchange for a full scholarship with guaranteed admittance to Northwestern, housing, a monthly allowance, and a large sum of money at the end of the contract. My employer had the option to renew the agreement yearly, and I had the choice not to sign for an additional year. If I chose not to renew, I was still entitled to continue my education at Northwestern, but I would be required to pay for all my expenses, including tuition. In return, I agreed to all the terms and conditions that my employer requested. Faithfulness to your employer was mandated. Also, once I signed the agreement, the decision of who I worked for was out of my hands.

My profile would be seen only by Karen until it was presented to those clients she deemed match-worthy. If the first benefactor chose another employee, my profile would remain open until Karen tried again with someone else.

The only clause to void the contract was physical abuse. Once reported, Infidelity would then review and confirm that such abuse took place. Sexual acts agreed to could not be considered a violation or abuse if they fell within the bounds of the contract. If claims of abuse were proven, the employee was entitled to keep all compensation paid as well as unfulfilled months of the contract. If no proof of physical violence was found, the employee would be required to fulfill the contract or repay any funds previously paid and void the contract.

The paper under the requirements was a detailed list of sexual and nonsexual limits. It was required to be completed and added to my profile, so Karen could match another possible employer. Karen never said sex was required, but the information would be pertinent in case a sexual relationship developed. It also lowered the risk of incompatibility. The four-page questionnaire asked about explicit and detailed sexual acts, including those of BDSM.

I spent the next few hours with my phone in one hand and the document in the other and researched as I read. Some of it I'd never even heard before. I marked each one with yes, soft or hard. The difference between hard and soft limits was one of the many things I learned with my research. The hard limits were the most important because it would include things I refused to perform or have done to me. I always knew sex sold, but until now, I hadn't grasped how much.

I didn't have enough sexual experience to know what I liked and didn't like. One night with a study partner was the only reference I had. We'd stayed up all night studying for finals and decided we should celebrate the next day. We headed to the beach for relaxation and fun. It was too cold to swim in the ocean, but the sun was bright as waves crashed the shore. Our fingers interlinked, and we took off running when water sprayed up and splashed us. Our hands were the first thing that connected but not the last. Our bodies molded together into a hug. One hug led to a kiss, and one kiss led to us naked in the backseat of his car on a deserted part of the beach. We'd spent so much time studying the last few weeks that I thought we both had feelings for one another. I was wrong. The only thing between us was the girlfriend he never mentioned. Heartbreak was just another hurdle I had learned to overcome.

No matter how Infidelity dressed it up, they sold sex; it was just called companionship. There was no way someone paid the insane amount of money these clients paid without some additional benefits to companionship. I almost guaranteed sex was that additional benefit. I needed to decide how badly I wanted Northwestern and if I would sell my soul and my body to an unknown person for one year for that goal.

I read all the documents, then read them again and

again until I knew them by heart. I knew that without this opportunity I wouldn't attend Northwestern.

As I sat there in the big bed, reviewing and completing the documents, Karen called to tell me I passed the interview and the examinations. How she was able to get all the test results, including lab work, in just a few hours was beyond me. This too must have been the norm for Infidelity's clientele.

She ended the conversation as usual: short and to the point. James would be at the hotel at eighty thirty in the morning to pick me up. The compensation for our meeting would be transferred to my account at that time. My decision would dictate if the interview progressed or not.

My mind overran with possibilities and what-ifs. I needed some fresh air to clear my head. Throwing on the more casual clothes I'd worn from home, I decided to walk in Central Park and think.

As I strolled, I thought about all of my dreams and all of the things that had gone wrong. I remembered the hurt I'd felt from the girls at the restaurant and from the rejection letter. I thought of my parents and what they would think if I signed an agreement to be owned. My mother and father had always supported and loved me. Their expectations were high, but they'd always been there for me. The loss of finances hadn't been their fault.

Would I have their support if they didn't think my choice was right?

I always considered my parents in every decision I made. I'd never wanted to hurt or disappoint them—I still didn't.

Then I thought about something they'd taught me.

Entering the competition wouldn't win me the race. You wouldn't get anywhere if you only showed up to the track. The only way to win and succeed was to take the first step, the second, and then the third. Each step along the road empowered the next until you reached accomplishments along the way. I'm sure they weren't referring to being a paid prostitute—or was *companion* the right word? But nevertheless, I applied the same principle to this situation. If I didn't take the next step, my dream could be gone forever.

The more I thought about my goals and dreams, the more I realized what I wanted in life. To some, it may be the walk of shame, but for me, it was liberating. And for the first time in my life, I didn't care what people thought. It was my fucking life, and it was about damn time I lived it for me. I hadn't planned it, but now the first step to my future and my dreams was Infidelity.

I'd managed hurdles. Now I had a possibility.

I was going to take it.

The world needed to fuck itself and let me finally be who I wanted to be—me.

The next morning, James picked me up at precisely eight thirty and drove me to Infidelity. Karen met me at the elevator and took me straight to her office.

"Melissa, have you made a decision?"

My voice was sure. "I want to sign."

"Good, do you have all the paperwork completed? Once everything is processed, you'll go downstairs for pictures."

Karen accepted all the paperwork I'd filled out the night before; glancing at it, she slid it into a file folder. My hand shook, and I felt nauseous as I looked at the contract in front of me. I blinked a few times and decided it was now or never.

I picked up the black pen off Karen's desk and scrolled my name across the places where she instructed me to. Every curve and stroke of my name on the dotted lines took me closer to my dream but also closer to the nightmare that possibly awaited me. Figuratively speaking, every i dotted and t crossed locked me into a new world. What I didn't know was if I was prepared to live in that new place.

Time would tell, and I could only hope for the best.

The next day, I flew home and waited for Karen to call. From that moment on, my life changed, and so did the way I viewed the world. My signing with Infidelity wasn't a sure thing to become a companion. It was just an opportunity to be chosen. Weeks after I returned from New York, I still hadn't heard from Karen. I started to think that maybe I wouldn't. Doubt crept back in.

I knew Karen had mentioned that placements usually took many months. However, if I wanted to register for spring classes, I didn't have months. Courses were limited, and I needed to sign up soon. It was as I struggled with the doubts of the spring semester that my phone rang, and the call had a New York area code.

"Hello," I said, answering my phone just as I reached my parked car.

"Miss Summers, your agreement has been picked up." I recognized Karen's voice. "Please remember that you signed an NDA. We will be in touch." That was all that was said before the line went dead.

I looked around; it felt like déjà vu. Had someone

waited to call me, watching me until I opened my car door? My gut told me that if I was being watched it was by Infidelity, but that reasoning didn't stop the fear that ran up my spine. I jumped in the car and locked the doors.

I spent the next week walking on eggshells. Food and sleep weren't in my thoughts, only questions.

Who bought the agreement? Was he handsome? How would he treat me?

So many questions...all with no answers.

I had to wait until they decided it was the right time. I just hoped I wouldn't lose my mind until that time came.

I finally calmed down enough to eat and sleep again, and an envelope magically appeared in the front seat of my car, again while my doors were locked. Sweat poured down my back as I reached for the thick paper. Panic set in.

This was real; I'd sold myself.

I would have sex with a complete stranger.

I prayed he wasn't old. Then I reconsidered. Maybe old was better. He wouldn't want sex because he wouldn't be able to get it up. Fuck, he probably takes that damn blue pill to stay hard for hours. Thoughts kept firing through my head. What if someone bought me to give to someone else?

What if...OMG, what the hell did I agree to?

I needed answers, and the only way to get them was to open the envelope. I pulled on the top, not even bothering with the red wax seal. I scanned the documents. It was just copies of what I signed and my letter of acceptance to Northwestern. I cried and laughed; between that, I screamed and yelled my excitement. Anyone who walked by my car would think I was insane. Hell, I might have been to take this risk, but I needed to follow the path I chose.

A white box was on the bottom of the envelope with a heart-shaped tag attached to the top.

MELISSA,

May this next year open more than doors—

I FLIPPED THE TOP OPEN. Inside was a gold necklace with a small diamond pendant in the shape of a key. I fingered the charm—it was beautiful. I pulled it out and fastened it around my neck. I wasn't sure how I could explain the necklace to my parents, so I tucked it under my shirt. They knew I saved every dime and would never splurge on jewelry. I had fed them enough lies already, so I chose avoidance instead.

CHAPTER 9

The Beginning of the End

Melissa

Two weeks after my agreement was bought, I loaded my car and headed to Evanston, Illinois, not far from Chicago. Karen said I wouldn't need to bring anything at all. All of my accommodations were prepared for my arrival. Closets and dressers overflowed with clothes in my size and my favorite toiletries. I had no idea who bought my agreement or what the person who bought it looked like, but he seemed to know an awful lot about me.

A handwritten note was placed on the counter for me to find, scripted by, I assumed, a man. It said he would arrive on Friday night, and next to the note was a cell phone. According to the letter, the iPhone was programmed with one number and no name. This phone was part of our agreement, according to the note; therefore, it wasn't to be used for anything but our communication. He didn't sign his name, just the salutation and a few lines about how he has waited a long time to find a match, but he knew I was the one the moment he saw me.

The apartment was fully furnished, yet bare of pictures and personal items. As empty as it was, it felt homey, or maybe I was just comforting myself. The apartment balcony overlooked a nature preserve with private access for the residents of the building. Tables and gazebos were situated to one side of a lake with paver sidewalks swirled on the grass. A wrought-iron fence enclosed the elaborate sanctuary and kept any nonresidents out.

I carried two phones now, the phone from my previous life and the one to my new. My old one rarely rang, and the iPhone had yet to. The first time the new phone went off, my pulse thumped, and my heart about stopped when the text message came through. I startled, and the phone almost fell to the ground when I tried to pick it up with shaky hands.

PRIVATE CALLER: **I will be there promptly at 8 p.m. I expect you have already explored the apartment and found the closet filled with clothes and the bathroom filled with all your toiletries. Pick out a pretty dress— get all dolled up for me. Be ready when I arrive.**
Me: Okay.

I KNEW I should have said more, but I couldn't think of anything else.

PRIVATE CALLER: **In the top drawer in the closet dresser, there are ties. Cover your eyes with one of my ties that matches the dress you plan to wear. No peeking.**

Five hours from now, I would meet the man with whom I'd spend the next year of my life. I showered, shaved, and fixed my hair and makeup. I slipped on a short black dress that barely covered my ass. At 7:45, I tied a solid black tie around my eyes and not so patiently waited. It was an eternity before he walked through that door.

With my eyes covered, I only had my other senses to depend upon. A strong scent of woodsy cologne with a hint of citrus filled the air. His shoes echoed through the apartment on the wood floors. One, two, three—then nothing. One, two, three and once again nothing. I didn't know how many steps it was from the door to the spot where I sat, but he intentionally drew it out. I didn't know where he was, but he was close—I sensed the heat from him.

I heard the hitch of his breath as his finger caressed my face. "Melissa, my beautiful Melissa. Do you know how long I've waited for you—how many times I imagined you on top of me?"

I tensed with his touch, but that didn't stop his fingers from tracing my face. His deep, masculine voice commanded my attention, and it was hard to focus on anything with him touching me. I also craved to see his face, the man who had waited for me to come along. If his voice was any indication of his looks, I won the fucking lottery. I needed to see him; slowly I reached up to remove the tie from around my eyes but was stopped.

"No, not yet. I don't want to ruin the surprise."

This time when he talked there was something about his voice… it seemed familiar. Even with my eyes covered, I felt his stare. "I can't believe you are finally mine."

"For—" The rest of my words went unsaid as he laid his finger on my lips.

"Melissa, I can stay only one night, then I have to get back home for an important meeting. I'll be back next week for a longer period. I'm afraid you'll be disappointed when you see me for the first time." He bent down and placed a soft kiss on my lips. "For tonight, I need you to keep your eyes covered." His fingers leisurely wandered from my lips, chin, and neck until they rested on the top of my breast. One finger caressed my nipple until each of his hands cupped my breasts and kneaded them through my clothes.

"Tonight, I want to get to know and touch every inch of your skin. Learn every one of your desires." His palm brushed my leg as one of his fingers slowly lifted the black flowered sundress higher until it bunched around my waist. He leaned in and pinned me to the back of the sofa.

"Fuck, you smell so good." His nose stroked my panties. He laid another soft kiss between my legs, and then he was gone.

"My sweet girl, come with me." His hand clasped around mine and led me toward the bedroom and then we came to a stop. "Don't move." Another kiss on my nose.

Something soft covered my head and rested against the

tie. "Keep your eyes closed. This will cover your eyes better." He turned me around as he secured the mask and removed the tie from my eyes. "I have a better use of the tie." He let out a little laugh. I swear, I felt his lip curl up into a smirk on my shoulder.

He twirled me around like a ballerina. "Tonight, I'll explore your body and mind. I'll allow you two questions, but it doesn't mean I'll answer. Things will be revealed soon enough."

He leaned his hips into me. He just revealed something to me without questions: his dick was massive, and he didn't have any issues getting hard.

The soft whispers that echoed in my ears made me crazy. "Melissa, I won't be fucking you tonight, but I will touch, caress, and taste you. Nothing more."

What the fuck? We hadn't even started anything, and I was already in need—something I didn't know I even had until this moment. My dress was lifted over my head, and his large hands cupped my breasts, massaging them. I was pulled closer into him as he reached around to unfasten my bra, letting it fall to the floor. Soft breath tickled me as he kissed my stomach and continued all the way the down to my pussy. He sucked and nipped at me through my panties before sliding his long fingers in the waistband and lowering them. I stood before him completely naked and wanting more of his touch.

"God, you are fucking gorgeous!"

His breath hitched as he placed his arms around me and positioned me in the center of the bed. He padded through the room before the bed dipped. He crawled up my body slowly, leaving the heat of his breath in his path. "Give me your hands."

His words were sexual and full of longing; the instinct to resist never had a chance. My body pleaded. I needed him to keep his promise to explore every inch of my body. "That's my girl. I'm not going to hurt you. I will be the only one touching tonight. You will get to explore my body soon enough."

One minute my hands lay on my stomach, and the next they were raised and secured to the headboard.

"Now that I have you, where should I start to taste you? I've been a fucking starved man for way too long. Damn, you're fucking gorgeous and worth every penny I paid to get you." He kissed me up and down my body as he spoke of his desires. My nipples pebbled, and chills ran up my spine. "Your pale milky-white skin against the dark sheets, your red hair fanned out across my pillows... I want to fuck you so badly. I made a promise: I wouldn't fuck you until you know who I am."

My body was on fire. His fingers and his tongue licked, touched, and embraced every inch of my body as he assured me he would. I needed more. My pussy pulsated with want.

"Do it—please, just fuck me." My mouth overtook and talked for my body, not my mind. I didn't even know his name. I knew eventually we would have sex but not within the first hour. I knew I should protest, beg for time to get to know him, but those words never left my mouth.

"My dirty girl, not tonight, but I promise soon."

"Please, I need—"

A finger was placed over my lips. "I know exactly what

you need, but I make the rules. Do I need to remind you who works for whom? I've read your hard limits very carefully. Punishment wasn't one of them." His voice dropped to just above a murmur as he nipped at my ear, his breath sweet like peppermint. "My sweet girl, remember punishment can be more than my hand turning your ass red. I have the option of turning your ass red and leaving you unsatisfied. Or maybe, I might just prefer to use my belt on your perky little ass until it is a nice crimson color. Then I'll stick my cock into your ass and fuck you while feeling the heat of your punished skin against me, my dick deep inside you and my balls slapping that sore ass of yours."

I should've been scared or appalled by the way he spoke. I should have screamed the *yellow* or maybe even *red* safe word from the agreement. He needed to be slapped for all the vile and disgusting words coming from his mouth. The thought that someone would fuck my ass scared the shit out of me. But more than that, it excited me. I didn't care what he did as long as I had a sexual release.

He tortured my body for hours, and at the end of the night, my body exploded with an orgasm that rocked my world. I was nothing more than a pile of flesh with no bones to support me.

"Sleep, my sweet Melissa."

I woke untied and naked with the blindfold still around my eyes. The apartment was silent but the smell of food and coffee filtered into the room. I slipped the blindfold away. Even before I had my sight, I felt his absence. I wandered out of the bedroom after I pulled one of his white undershirts over my head. A serving tray with a coffee urn and domed plate was set on the counter. A little note was atop the dome of what I assumed covered my breakfast. This man was going to be my death. After last night I needed more. He teased and satisfied more without actual sex than I thought it possible.

MY SWEET MELISSA,

I have fantasized about your body for a very long time. My fantasies of you paled in comparison to touching and tasting your delicious body. I wanted to eat you all over again this morning, but I had an unavoidable appointment.

My dick hasn't stopped begging for you, just as your pussy begged and pleaded with me last night. I wish last night didn't have to end. The memories will keep my hand very busy. Fuck, the thought of you on my tongue makes me hard all over.

I will be gone for a few days, but arranged to work from here next week. We will discuss all my wants and expectations that I require you to fulfill. I had anticipated we would resolve everything last night, but once I saw you, my determination not to touch you was overruled by my desire to sample you.

I ordered your breakfast. Rest until Monday; you will need your energy.

I will text your instructions.

CHAPTER 10

Revelations

Melissa

Saturday and Sunday were slow and uneventful. I walked along the lake in the nature reserve and went into town to wander and explore. I was bored. I had already registered, and classes hadn't started yet at Northwestern, so I had nothing to do but wait for his arrival. I still hadn't heard from him when I woke up on Monday morning. I knew he said he would be back today, but I had no idea what time.

I laid the iPhone on the coffee table and waited. Nothing happened. Then I decided I needed to do something that inevitably would cause the phone to ring. I watched fifteen minutes of a movie before I decided to take a nap. When that didn't work, I went to take a bath. I grabbed the iPhone and set it on the counter. Filled the tub, shaved, and even soaked in the warm water until it turned cold. The phone still wouldn't ring. I gave up on trying to make it ring and threw it on the coffee table and went to the kitchen to fix a drink.

That was when it happened.

The phone pinged, and I ran toward the living room. Fuck, I should have tried that first. I tripped and slid across the hardwood floors into the couch arm.

PRIVATE NUMBER: **Be on the couch tonight at six o'clock.**

Me: Yes, Sir.

Private number: Fuck. Tonight, I make you mine.

Me: Promise? My pussy's been hungry.

Private number: Don't fucking touch! It's mine. Be on couch at six o'clock. Wear a matching set of bra and panties. Match one of my ties and put it over your eyes.

Me: Do you have a color preference?

Private number: White would make you look like an angel sent to take me to heaven. Red or black would turn you into the she-devil herself, sent to take me straight to hell.

Me: Sooooo... do you want heaven or hell?

Private number: Surprise me—am so fucking hard right now. You pick the color. My dick will decide if we go to heaven or hell.

Me: I'll be waiting for you—in hell.

Private number: Fuck! My decision, not yours. I promise when we're done, you'll be in fucking heaven and I'll be sent to hell.

Holy shit. I didn't know where I got the courage to respond like that. I didn't know anything about the man I was provoking. I just knew that on Friday he gave me something I hadn't realized I missed—the need to be wanted. I'd had urges in the past but nothing like the desire he awoke in me. Not only did my body feel alive, but for the first time ever, *I* felt alive.

At 5:50, I sat on the couch in my bra and panties, blind-folded with one of his ties. I tried on every set of undergarments in the drawer until I settled on a red silky G-string and a matching red low-cut satin bra trimmed in black lace. His tie was the perfect match, black silk with thick red lines cut at an angle. I didn't want to be fucked like an angel. I wanted to be fucked like the she-devil forged in the fire by Satan himself, a man who could make me desperate with need with just his words.

The door opened, and his scent and presence filled the room. I heard his shoes against the wood floors, and then they stopped, and the only sound was our breathing, both deep and hard.

I smiled, sensing that he liked what he saw.

"Well, someone seems proud of her attire." Desire and need saturated his voice.

"Does Sir like it?"

Footsteps slammed against the floor, and before I knew it, I was pinned between the couch and his hard body. His mouth covered mine as he sucked every breath out of me, leaving me gasping. Large hands held my wrists, his legs straddled mine, and his other hand grabbed and caressed my breasts. I wasn't able to see, but fuck, I could feel his massive dick pressed against me. Each time his tongue swept through my mouth, his dick pushed harder against my clit. My body was no longer mine but his to play with as he pleased. I was nothing more than clay for his sculptor hands to mold.

"Fuck me," he said, standing. Before I knew it, he picked me up and carried me to the bedroom. "Melissa, I said I wanted you to see me, to know who you were fucking before I took you." He placed me on the bed and covered me with his body. Soft little kisses were placed all over me. "Don't move."

I didn't care who he was at the moment; all I cared about was his cock. For all I knew, he was a serial killer, but as long as he fucked me before he killed me, at that moment, I didn't care. "I don't care who you are. Please touch me."

His presence disappeared, and I immediately missed his weight pressed against me. The scent of his cologne surrounded me, and the sound of a crinkling bag alerted me to his return. My right arm was lifted and placed into a cloth loop and then the left, both secured to the bed frame. Sharp teeth scraped my skin as he nibbled my stomach. In a quick motion, I felt him grab my panties in his mouth and pull them down each leg slowly with soft kisses along the way. Then my legs were secured but spread-eagled instead of looped together. It made my need even stronger with no way to squeeze my thighs together. The bed dipped, and hands roamed up and down my body.

"I need to fuck you. I can't wait any longer."

Long fingers stroked me and pumped into me and then just stopped. Desperation for more made me beg. "More.

Please." I didn't need to beg for long before he smashed into me with such force that I cried out.

"Sorry, baby."

The pain turned to pleasure as he continued his delicious attack on my body. His dick was thick and filled me in ways I never knew were possible—the restraints were the only thing that kept me in place as he slammed into me. His mouth moved between my lips and breasts while his hands roamed my body. One soft touch before he squeezed every part of me. He drove me crazy, but it was his moans that pushed me over and made me come hard. Once he let out his final moan and shot his cum into me, exhaustion took over. As much as I wanted to see the man who rocked my world, learning his identity would have to wait until I was coherent again.

I don't know how long I slept. But when I woke, my arms were still secured to the bed and my eyes were still covered with the blindfold. The only change was that while I slept, he'd unfastened my legs. My consciousness grew more acute as fingers brushed my skin, ever so lightly, leaving goose bumps in their wake.

"Morning, my sweet girl."

"Morning."

"I've decided to keep you tied up while we talk." His fingers continued to trace every inch of me. "Melissa, regardless of your feelings, you're mine for the next year. I can enforce the contract, including the companionship, but I want you to want to be here."

His fingers moved from my breast to my hairline, and slowly he inched the tie off my eyes. My vision blurred. I blinked them into focus.

"What the fuck—why?" I pulled my arms and kicked my legs wildly. Fear and pain struck me. I felt nauseous. No, this couldn't be true. He was—fucking hell. This wasn't possible.

"Why? Why would you do this." Tears ran down my face, hurt filled my heart. I just fucked Peyton Harrison, my mother's best friend's husband, a man twice my age. "Get the fuck off me. Get off. What the hell is wrong with you? Oh my God."

"Melissa, I'm sure this is a shock."

"Shock? You think this is a fucking shock? It's more than a shock." My legs kicked at him. "I just fucked you. Regina has been like an aunt to me, and I just fucked her husband."

Anger overcame him. "I own you for the next year. I will fuck you when and where I want. I paid a lot of money for you. Hell, more than most. I don't need to explain myself, but I will—this once—after you stop this fucking tantrum."

"Fuck you! Untie me now. I—"

My sentence was cut off and my body flipped over. The next thing I felt was his hand smacking my bare ass over and over. My tears turned to screams as my ass burned. Finally, he shifted me to my side and pulled me into his embrace after the last slap. My back was to his front and his hard cock was pressed against my sore ass. I thought of his threat of fucking my ass after he beat it and tensed as I tried to move forward.

"I won't fuck you again until you're ready, but that doesn't mean I won't punish you for being disrespectful. YOU. ARE. MINE."

"Why? Tell me why." I'm not sure how he understood me through all the tears and bumbling.

"Rest now, and we'll talk when you calm down." His voice became soft and patient as he stroked my hair.

The next time I woke up, my arms were untied, and Peyton wasn't in bed. His dress shirt was hanging over the chair, and I slipped it on before I went to find him. Slowly, I made my way through the apartment. I found him sitting at the dining room table with his computer opened and a cup of coffee. As pissed as I was, I still thought he looked hot as hell in his lounge pants and no shirt. I tried not to stare, but damn, without my knowing it, he'd wormed his way into my daily thoughts and fantasies since the first night he touched me.

"Morning. Would you like coffee?"

"Please."

"Come sit with me, and we'll talk."

He went into the kitchen and brought a cup of coffee for me and refreshed his own. It didn't take long for me to remember my sore ass when I sat on the hard cherry-wood chair. Jumping up, I rubbed my ass.

"Melissa, I said to sit with me."

"I would rather stand. Please?" I added the last part as I remembered his warning about being respectful.

He cocked his eye at me as a warning to obey.

I evened my tone, drawing out my request. "May we please sit on the couch?"

He snickered, nodded, and gestured for me to go first as he picked up our coffee mugs. I still needed to keep my distance from him. Therefore, I gingerly sat at one end of the couch as far away as possible. It still hurt to sit on the soft cushions, but not nearly as badly as it did on the wooden chair.

Peyton and I talked for a couple of hours. At first, he spoke, and I pretended to listen. I didn't want to care what he had to say. However, the longer I sat there, the more things made sense. I wasn't sure if I'd stopped pretending to hear or pretending not to listen because his words began to filter into me.

"Melissa, the first time I saw you, I didn't know who you were or that you were only sixteen. All I saw was a wild redhead who I wanted to tame. When I realized who you were, it was like a knife going through my heart." He stopped and waited for a response.

I didn't have one. I knew when we met that I felt something. I also knew that at the dinner the night after my graduation, there had been a connection. I thought what I'd felt was a kid with a crush on an older man. I didn't want to admit that even though I hadn't seen him since that dinner, I'd thought of him often. Taking my eyes away from my empty coffee mug, I glanced over and looked at him.

Really looked at him.

Our gazes met as I stared into the eyes I wanted to hate, but didn't, into the eyes of the man who would probably ruin me. I replayed in my head the words he'd said. He wanted to tame the wild redheaded girl. He desired me. He needed to be with me. Never did I hear that he wanted me in his life, only that he fantasized about me in his bed.

I wondered if he'd still want me after I was tamed. I also wondered how long it would be until he was done taming me, and he moved on.

I knew if I continued this agreement, I would spend the rest of my life in lies and deceit. Holidays and birthdays with Regina would never be the same. Even though I rarely saw Peyton when Regina was around, I would know that she slept in his bed when he was home and that I slept with him when he wasn't. Would I be able to handle his rejection at the end of our agreement? We both knew this couldn't go further.

But in reality, none of that really mattered.

I'd signed an agreement, and he'd bought it. It was simple, despite how complex. Peyton owned me for the next year. As we spoke, I contemplated my option to break the NDA and tell my parents and Regina the truth, but what would that choice cost me? The other possibility was to live my life for me, go through with what I'd started, and finish the road I'd chosen to travel.

I hated the notion that deception and betrayals would take over my life, but in reality, hadn't they already? From the time I received the first invitation to Infidelity, it was one lie after another. The charade he played pissed me off, yet I still felt something. For the first time in my life, I felt what it was like to live for me and not someone else's expectations.

Unfortunately, I would find out soon enough that I still had expectations to live by, and despite my current sense of liberation, this path had never really been my decision.

Again, I glanced over and looked at him. As I did, I knew I wanted to experience more with him. I was livid with the situation, but with the way my body responded to him, my desires were stronger than my anger.

"Melissa, I knew it was wrong. Fuck, you were sixteen

years old." He shook his head. "I tried to forget you, but nothing worked. No matter how many people I fucked, all I saw was you."

"What? What about Regina? Don't you love her?"

"No."

I had trouble understanding what he was saying. "Then why? Why would you marry her?"

"Regina and I have an arrangement. It has only been the last few years that she wanted a real marriage. She's cheated on me as much as I've cheated on her. Hell, she probably still is. She's probably with someone now."

"Why stay married?" I asked earnestly.

"It's a long story, but it's fair to say that we use each other."

Peyton and I talked the rest of the day. That night we went to bed without any physical contact. The next few days were much the same. Despite the lack of contact, we continued to talk while we walked along the paths through the park and Northwestern. Our conversations went in many different directions. He asked why I wanted to go Northwestern and what I wanted in the future. He listened. The only thing we didn't talk about was him. He stayed attentive and caring but reserved.

The night before he left, I was reminded that this was an arrangement and certain expectations were my obligation to meet. When he called, I must answer. When he was in town, I was at his complete disposal. In the bedroom, I would be his submissive. Punishments for misbehavior would be enforced, and he would determine the severity. He owned me. I wasn't allowed to flirt, tease, or date. The punishment for the latter would be accessed not only by him but also by Infidelity. My dismissal was just one aspect of a possible penalty. I wasn't sure I liked the way that sounded, but it wasn't like they could kill me.

CHAPTER 11

Following the Path

Melissa

The next few months were the best time of my life. Twice a week I attended classes at Northwestern and studied regularly to keep my grades up. Even though Infidelity guaranteed my acceptance, I wasn't about to lose another scholarship. Peyton visited two to three days a week. Most of the time we were together was spent in the apartment. Once in a while, we went on walks or had a picnic by the lake, the basket filled with cheeses, fruits, crackers, and something sweet for dessert. A couple of times, Peyton slipped a cold bottle of wine in the basket to have with our lunch. It didn't matter that I was only eighteen. All that mattered was the fun we had after I drank too much.

The sex between us was hot. Peyton enjoyed finding a

reason to punish me, and I went out of my way for the punishment. His punishments took me to ecstasy. I learned the best way to incite his wrath was to send pictures of myself in lingerie. That was guaranteed to earn me a spanking by his magical hands.

"Lie across the bed. Five with my belt."

He rarely used his belt, but when he did, I came harder than ever. Peyton never just slapped my ass when he punished; no, he'd rub his fingers through the crease of my ass and then dip his long digits into my pussy. He'd pump his fingers until I was dripping, then suck my juices off of them. "Fuck, you taste like heaven."

One night, I lay naked on the bed, face down, with my wrists looped into the straps attached to the headboard and each leg shackled to the post of the footboard. Next, Peyton blindfolded my eyes with the mask before he licked up and down my body.

He had a plan. I just didn't know what it was yet.

One minute it was his tongue, and the next, the sting of his belt. After three lashes with the belt, he licked the welts on my ass. God, as bad as the belt hurt, his touch and tongue made me crazy. Two more swats and I needed something to help ease the pressure in my pussy. Sometime during the exercise, I'd managed to bunch the sheets under me in a ball and pushed into them for a little friction. Since I'd heard padded footsteps head toward the bathroom, I pushed even harder into the sheets, thinking he wouldn't see. My ass was already on fire when the whoosh of the belt came across my ass again.

Whack.

"Fuck."

"Bad girls get punished, not rewarded. Did you think I didn't notice your pussy flexing and your ass squeezing together? Here your punishment was over, and now we have a whole other transgression. Naughty, naughty." His tone was playful. "You tried to take my enjoyment away."

"Please fuck me. My pussy is aching with need."

"Sunshine, there will be no reward for you tonight. Maybe I'll leave you tied up all night, so you don't touch yourself. You need to learn your lesson."

"Peyton, please, I'll do anything, please."

"Anything, huh. How badly do you want to come?"

"I'll do anything, please."

"Another punishment?"

"Yes! Yes! Whatever you want, just let me come." My body had more control over my mouth than my brain did. I didn't think my ass would be able to take much more. I was ready to scream the safe word when he caressed me softly. He knew what he was doing. He would put me on edge to safe word him, and then pleasure me, so I wouldn't. A chill from the air conditioning skirted across my skin, yet did nothing to cool the fire on my ass.

Peyton bent down. I couldn't see him, but the peppermint breath said he was right in front of me. "I'll let you choose your punishment, but once you've made a decision, it can't be changed. Understood?"

"Yes." Desire laced my voice. "Sir." A hiccup bubbled out.

"Now your choices."

"One. You lie here all night unsatisfied, and I pleasure myself. After I shoot my load all over your sexy-as-fuck body, your mouth will be filled with my dick to add to my pleasure, but you will not be allowed any relief."

He ran his fingers up and down the crease of my ass and along what I assumed were welts from his belt. Slowly he slid a finger into me.

"Sweetheart, your pussy must really love my belt—you're wet as hell. And so is the sheet."

He was right. As bad as the belt hurt, I craved it.

"Two."

"Please." I wasn't sure how much longer I would be able to go without relief.

"Two, I bend you over the bed, and spank your fine ass again. I'll be generous since your ass is already welted from my belt. Three more with my belt and then ten with my hand.

"Two!" I wiggled and squirmed on the mattress, and his hand came down on my ass.

"Are you sure because I didn't finish what that option two entailed."

With my body aching from need, I didn't care what else the option entailed as long as he would let me come. "Please, do whatever you want as long as I can come. Please." I wasn't ashamed to beg. Honestly, I wasn't sure what I agreed to. I probably wouldn't have agreed with what he had planned if I hadn't been so desperate.

"Okay."

He stood up and unshackled me. "Stand up straight, hands in the air. No touching."

I stood up straight with my hands in the air as he pulled the restraints around the bed. My legs were fastened together, and there was a long cord connected to the wrist restraints that he dragged under the bed. He moved something around before he came back to me.

"Walk toward the bed. Closer. Good, now lean down with your arms over your head." Soft pillows sat at the edge of the bed to hold my ass in the air. There must have been at least two the way my body angled toward the bed. My wrists were placed in the loops, and he pulled it tight. With my arms and legs secured with the bungee cord, I was trapped in place.

"Blindfold or no blindfold?"

"Blindfold." I wasn't sure if I wanted to see what he had planned for me; plus, it always added to the anticipation. Peyton leaned over me and leaned his dick into my ass.

He tapped my lips with his finger. "Open."

My mouth opened, and he shoved the sheet that had been bunched under me in it. "Suck on the sheets your greedy pussy used."

My mind and body were on sensory overload. I felt something cold drip down the crack of my ass and then his finger slide into my puckered hole. My ass clenched automatically.

"Relax. It will only hurt for a minute. I need to prepare you for the second part of your punishment."

I exhaled a breath through my nose and tried with all my might to relax. From what I had read, the more relaxed, the easier it slides in.

"Push back and relax."

I felt more cold goo drip on whatever pressed against the rim of my hole. Another push and my ass filled with something. It was cool and felt strange as it slid in.

"It's a butt plug," Peyton said as he moved it in and out, stretching me.

The pain subsided once he had it firmly seated in my ass. It wasn't enjoyable but tolerable. Peyton leaned over me again, placing pressure on the plug.

"Now, the first part of your punishment is the butt plug. You're not to move. Do you understand?"

I couldn't answer. My arms and legs were immobile, and my mouth was occupied with the sheets saturated from my earlier desire. I couldn't imagine how I looked with my ass in the air and the toy sticking out of my cheeks. The next thing I heard was the chair from the corner scraping on the floor behind me, followed by the sound of Peyton lowering his zipper.

"Melissa, you look beautiful. It's a shame my dick has to be satisfied with my hand."

Though I couldn't speak, my pussy begged and pleaded for him to satisfy me. I needed to come—he promised to let me come. A final grunt filled the air as his hot cum squirted over me. He rubbed his fingers through the cum and swirled it all around my back and ass.

"Sweetheart, your cunt is dripping all over the floor. Maybe I should make you lick it up too, once I'm done fucking you."

Screams of pleasure were muffled by the sheet and replaced with moans. The only thing I could do was squirm and squeeze against the plug inserted into my ass, but nothing helped or eased my need. I wasn't sure how long I stayed that way. I was about to give up when fire once again flashed across my ass.

"Melissa, normally I would have you count, but your mouth is full."

Two more strikes across my ass with the belt, then it dropped to the floor. His hand took over slapping my ass over and over. Each blow sent the butt plug deeper into my ass. Tears sprang and dripped down my cheeks. I wasn't sure if it was from the pain or pleasure, but I refused to release the sheet from my mouth. Relief overtook me and my ass when he finally stopped.

"Your ass is so beautiful. The red welts lining your perfect ass and the butt plug wedged between your perfect cheeks makes me even harder."

His hands danced across my backside and turned the butt plug several times before his dick slammed into my pussy hard. It was the strangest feeling; my ass burned and plugged and a mouth full with my own desire as Peyton thrust in and out of my pussy. I'd never felt so full. I was seconds from release when he stilled. I wanted to scream and shout for him to continue, but this was my punishment for taking away his pleasure.

Peyton pet my head as he removed the plug. "You took the first part of your punishment like a good girl, so I've decided you deserve a reward. But first, I get my reward and the rest of your punishment. It's time for your ass to meet my dick."

Peyton lined up his dick, pushed in, and repeated the in-and-out motion. A sudden pain flashed through my ass, passing once he fully seated himself inside me. My eyes rolled back, and ecstasy took over. He reached around and rubbed my clit until we both came.

The only thing that kept me on my feet were the

restraints. When we were both satisfied, I was satiated and thoroughly exhausted. My body lost all tension. I couldn't stand if I wanted. It was then that Peyton threw the pillows toward the headboard, untied me, lifted me into his arms, and placed me in the center of the mattress. I felt the bed dip as he pulled my limp body to him. My head lay on his chest with my arm over his stomach.

"Sleep, sweet girl."

"Peyton."

"Yes?"

"I love you."

CHAPTER 12

Loneliness

Melissa

I didn't know it at the time, but that night changed everything, or maybe it was those three little words. I thought it was my imagination that he tensed when I declared my feelings for him. I should've figured out that something was wrong when Peyton was gone the next morning, leaving me with only a quick note on the table that something came up, and he needed to get back to Myrtle Beach.

What did he think would happen when I was all alone with no friends?

He became my everything. I hadn't much of a chance to meet people with all the time I spent with him and on my classes.

For the next few weeks, Peyton canceled his visits—

company emergencies. I remembered those were the same words he used to Regina when he didn't want to be home. I guessed the saying karma's a bitch was right because now he said the same thing to me. I wondered how long until he decided he wanted his money's worth from me and how he would take it. The question was answered a few weeks later when I received a text from him. It was simple and to the point: he would be in town and needed my services. He actually said *services*. I was no longer the valued companion —I was the high-priced whore.

The next two months, Peyton stopped in for a few hours on three different visits. Each time he arrived at the apartment, took me straight to the bedroom, and fucked me. No play time, nothing extra. One time he didn't even bother to take off his clothes. I was leaned over the bed, fucked, and then he pulled his pants up and left. He was becoming even more detached with every visit.

Each day I sunk a little deeper into myself. I had distanced myself from my parents, ashamed of all the lies and on constant edge that I would allow something to slip. We still talked but not as much. I was too busy with my studies... at least that is what I led them to believe.

One day, I checked my phone after class and found a text from Peyton. It had been almost a month since his last visit. This text was different than the previous few that said to meet him at the apartment.

PEYTON: **Come home right after class—I need you.**

MY HEART PUMPED FASTER, and my body ached for him. He said he needed me. When I rushed back to the apartment, I found him in the bedroom naked, waiting for me. His clothes were thrown over the bed but he was sitting on the chair in the corner. His hand covered his dick as he slowly pumped it. It was one of the sexiest positions, him on display for me.

"On your knees and suck my dick."

There was something in his voice that made me hesitate.

"Now, Melissa!"

I dropped to my knees as he had taught me. My hands behind my back and my mouth open and ready. I leaned into him and swallowed his length as far as I could. Peyton began to flex and pump deeper and deeper until I gagged. Instinctively, I pushed my hands forward to push away. That was a mistake. He grabbed my hands, pulling me up as he stood. He threw me on the bed and tied my hands to the loops at the headboard. Then he crawled on top of me and sat on my chest.

"Didn't I tell you not to use your hands? Now it's time you learn to obey," he said with gritted teeth. "I'm not here to play, Melissa. I paid for you to suck my dick. Now fucking open your mouth and suck it."

Peyton shoved his dick into my mouth as far as he could and held it there until I gasped for air. Tears sprang from my eyes and fell to my pillow as he continued to thrust into my mouth over and over. It wasn't until I was about to pass out when Peyton finally stopped. He groaned as he pulled his dick out of my mouth and shot his cum all over my face.

"Eat it all." He pushed his cum into my mouth and held it shut until I swallowed. Next, Peyton unpinned me and sat to the side; he put his hand up my skirt and shoved his finger into me. "You really are a dirty whore, aren't you? Your pussy is always in need. Wet, willing, and ready to be fucked. I wonder what your parents and Regina would think if they saw little Miss Perfect now."

The coldness and calculating look in his eyes chilled me. I didn't know what I wanted, or maybe I did. My body craved to be sexually satisfied, but my heart required more. It begged to be loved, wanted, and needed.

Peyton leaned over and untied my hands, then opened the nightstand drawer and threw something down on the bed. "I can't stay, but I'm in a giving mood."

He turned, grabbed his clothes, and walked out of the bedroom. I reached over and picked up what he had thrown at me—a fucking dildo. The only place I wanted to stick that thing was his ass. The anger I felt was short-lived and turned to pain—one I had never felt.

A few minutes later, the door slammed shut and so did my heart.

I closed my eyes and rolled on my side, hugging the only thing willing to dry my tears, a pillow that lingered with Peyton's cologne. I cried for hours until there was nothing left in me. I decided, once again, that it was time to live for me and fuck the rest of the world and their rules.

Weeks passed since that night Peyton decided to discard me again, and each day I became more bored. Lonelier. There were still over six months on the contract that I had to honor. I signed to be a "companion" and from this point on that was all he would get from me. I wouldn't let him have any more of me emotionally.

I swore that night that I didn't care, and I would live my life, but the reality was that I was devastated. The following weeks the only thing I did was go to school and study. As the loneliness grew, so did my need for interaction with people.

I still hadn't heard from Peyton since the night he walked out and shattered my heart. I pulled out my books to study for my upcoming class exam and found an invitation to a club a few blocks up the street. I fidgeted with the necklace Peyton gave me before we started the arrangement. I argued with myself about whether I should go or not. One minute, I was studying and the next, I was in the bathroom getting dolled up for a night on the town. I needed to stop feeling sorry for myself. I told myself that it was just like when I lost the scholarship and started to live again. Peyton didn't care about me, so why should I care about him or his wants?

I questioned my decision multiple times after I headed toward the new dance club in town, *Final Stand*. The line to enter was long, and it took about an hour for me to reach the bouncer. He handed me back my license and opened the rope for me to enter. It was like nothing I had ever seen. Bright, colorful lights sparkled off all the people moving to the beat of the music. Above the wooden dance floor was a loft filled with people looking below. The upper level was the royalty and the lower their subjects to honor them.

For the first time in months, I actually felt young as the music pumped through my body. I realized that I had spent my teenage years working so hard to be an adult. I forgot that I was only eighteen. I found a little table in the corner away from the crowds and just watched. As much as I wanted to join the fun, I wasn't ready to break all of Peyton's rules.

A waitress dressed in a French-Maid outfit approached me. "Do you have a band?"

I lifted my right hand, no band. Only people twenty-one and over received the bands. It made it easier to identify the underaged patrons.

"What can I get for you?"

"Coke, please."

The waitress returned a few minutes later and placed a small shot glass on the table, and I looked up at the waitress with a confused look. "I ordered a Coke."

"It was sent from the gentleman upstairs."

This wasn't the Coke I ordered; it was alcohol. "What is it?" I lifted my arm and showed her I didn't have a band.

"It looks like a small cup of Coke." Her reply was short and annoyed. "At least that is what the gentleman who sent it said."

My eyes scrunched together, and I tilted my head. "But..."

Miss Attitude cut me off. "Look, I was told to bring you a drink. Drink it or don't. I have things to do." She turned around and left.

I stared at the drink and contemplated whether I wanted to try it or not. I had a glass of wine occasionally on holidays with my parents, but this shit was the strong stuff. One small sip and my eyes rolled back in my head, and my throat was on fire.

"Hello, beautiful."

I was startled when a sexy-as-hell male voice echoed. He picked up a long strand of my auburn hair and twirled it around his finger. His blue eyes locked on mine as he tucked the strand behind my ear. "My name is Bryce. What's your name, pretty lady?"

"Melissa. My name is Melissa." I stuttered. The pitch in my voice became higher as he rubbed his hand up and down my ivory skin as I spoke to him. My stomach flip-flopped, but I wasn't sure if it was the way he approached or the fact that he was the forbidden fruit that I wasn't allowed to taste. I knew the rules—I read the contract before I signed it—but I was lonely. I was tired of being alone, locked in a posh prison and treated like a whore. I just wanted to have fun for one night, to kick back and enjoy life.

"It's nice to meet you, Melissa. Well, I think we should take this party upstairs where the fun is. Besides, I have lots more where that came from." His head nodded toward the drink in my hand.

"Oh, you're the one who sent my drink? The waitress didn't tell me who." I felt even more electrified as he tucked my hair behind my ear, and his finger dallied on my shoulder.

His eyes beamed and his smile made my nipples pebble. I leaned in close to press my breast against his chest. I knew this was wrong, but the passion in his touch made me crave more. He held me closer, swagging our bodies to the music overhead. My body hummed at his touch; I knew I needed to get out before I did something I would regret.

Our eyes danced together as we studied each other but never uttered a word. Bryce reached for my hand before he brought it up to his lips for a soft and tender kiss. His lips were hot and sent sparks down my spine. I'm not sure if it was the excitement of being out or if he really made me feel things.

He must have sensed my uncertainty about leaving with him because he leaned down and whispered in my ear, "Sweet Melissa, don't you feel the connection? The spark when we touch?" His cologne was strong yet sensual, and when he talked to me, I could smell the cinnamon and alcohol on his breath.

My mind said no, but my body refused to listen. Once again, my body ruled my actions. Bryce decided my fate when our fingers interlocked, and I followed him up the stairs.

As much as my mind tried to convince my body to do otherwise, it was as if I wasn't in control anymore. We reached the top where a large man stood guard, but the minute he saw Bryce, he moved aside. Bryce emanated power and arrogance. He didn't wait for others; they waited on him. Bryce led me to a small table and pulled out a chair for me.

"I'll be right back."

The fog of Bryce's cologne vanished when he stepped away and allowed my mind to clear. I needed to get the hell out of there. I'd already broken more rules in one night then I had in all the months I'd been with Peyton. I hadn't technically done anything wrong, but if this party continued, I would.

"Bryce, I need to go…"

"Sweet Melissa, don't go. You'll break my heart."

"I have to," I protested. "If my friend finds out I'm here, he won't be happy."

"He? You have a boyfriend, Melissa, who let you out of his sight? He must be a damn fool. If you were mine, I'd never let you out of my sight."

"No. Yes. It just…" Once again I was at a loss as to how I could explain who Peyton was. Besides, if I told the truth, I would have to explain I was paid to be a companion and have sex with him.

"Sweet Melissa, I had plans for us. Big plans." He cupped my breasts and massaged them tenderly. My panties were soaked, and if I didn't get out of there fast, the world would be able to smell my arousal.

"Please, I really have to go."

Bryce didn't look happy, but he finally stepped away and toward the guard standing at the top of the stairs. He whispered something to him before he turned back to me. "Raul will make sure you get home." His next words came out as a command. I shouldn't have liked it, but I did. "Friday night, eight o'clock, meet me here."

CHAPTER 13

Breaking the Rules

Melissa

The next week, I studied and spent time alone without any contact from Peyton. I decided that if I hadn't heard from him by Friday morning, I would meet Bryce at the club. I knew I wasn't supposed to date, but I'd convinced myself that it wasn't a date. It was simply friends hanging out together. Peyton had developed a pattern, and his visits correlated with his payments. When I received money, he received a service. By that standard, this month's transaction had already occurred. If he stayed true to the schedule, he wouldn't be back for another two weeks.

This time when I arrived at *Final Stand*, Raul was at the door and ushered me into the club. I didn't have to wait or show my ID. He just slipped the white band on my arm and led me to the loft. A second bouncer opened the rope before I even uttered a word.

As I climbed the stairs, Bryce stood at the top with a drink in his hand. He was dressed even sexier than the last time I saw him: dark blue jeans and solid black dress shirt untucked from his pants. The first three buttons were undone, and a gold necklace hung from his neck.

Bryce took my hand and kissed my cheek. "I'm glad you came."

He led me to the same table from the week before. I hadn't noticed the view the last time I had been there. The entire bottom of the loft was made of glass and allowed the dance floor and bar to be viewed from above. I often wondered how he found me in the back of the club at a small table if he partied up here. He apparently had the perfect view. We drank and watched the dancers below for the first hour, and then he pulled me close to his body. His arms wrapped around me, and my head fell to his shoulder as we swayed to the music. The club music was pumping loud and to a fast beat, but our bodies moved in harmony with each other. It was like we had music just for us. One minute we were dancing, and the next our lips collided, and passion took over. His tongue swept into my mouth, taking my tongue hostage, sucking and pulling it into his mouth. His hands moved from my arms to the back of my head and tilted it to have better access. His kiss was a match, and I was the unlit candle—together combustible. My heart was beating faster, and my panties had just melted off of my body. Someone called his name and broke the connection; he groaned in annoyance.

"I'll be right back."

"Okay."

As he stepped away, all my senses came back. I realized the consequences if I didn't get out of there fast. It would cost me everything.

"Bryce, I need to go."

"But the party is just starting."

"I can't. If I get caught with you, I'll lose everything."

A smirk crossed his face. "Oh, I can make you lose everything with just my tongue."

Damn, why did he have to be so sexy? Turning him down wouldn't be easy. "I really have to go."

"Oh, Melissa, you break my heart and leave me desperate." He grabbed my hands and pulled me back. "Talk to me. Let me help you."

I leaned my head into his chest and inhaled; his scent alone made me weak again. He pulled me into another passionate kiss and was relentless with the attack on my mouth. His tongue worked fast as his hands pulled me even closer.

"Meet me tomorrow for lunch."

"I can't. I shouldn't be here now."

"Melissa, my sweet Melissa—please?"

"I'll think about it."

He took the phone out of my hand and called his phone. "I'll text you."

Fuck, I was in such a sex-induced haze, I didn't realize Bryce used the phone Peyton had given me. I needed to get away fast before I lost my will to leave.

"Fine. Where?"

"I'll pick you up tomorrow at noon. I'll take you somewhere we can talk and really get to know each other."

I knew it was against the rules, but I was so tired of being lonely and depressed. Bryce made me feel alive again. He treated me like Peyton did in the beginning—made me feel wanted. Our first lunch was simple and easy. We talked about school and our dreams. He spoke about his mother in Savannah, and that one day he would be the head of Montague Corporation. He told me about his childhood and that his mom had been the best friend of the corporation's owner and his mother's friend's husband had groomed him from a young age to take over the business. He would return to Savannah after graduate school and in no time at all be running a multimillion-dollar company. He never showed disapproval of the fact that I didn't come from money. He didn't care.

It wasn't until our last lunch that I realized Bryce cared about only one thing—his dick. Up until that time, Bryce had been one of the most charming men I'd ever met. He'd held my hand and kissed the top of my head like I was special. He'd never mentioned sex and never pushed for more.

Bryce always wore a gold chain, but this was the first time I noticed a charm with the letter "A" dangling from it. I tried to pick it up, but he twisted my arm back and squeezed tighter.

He growled, "Don't fucking touch!"

"Bryce, you're hurting me."

Just as fast as he turned angry, his demeanor changed again. "Melissa, I'm so sorry. I didn't mean to hurt you. It's just that the charm is special. It belongs to a... friend."

"Oh," I said. "I just wanted to look at it. It's beautiful. What does the "A" stand for?"

"Alexandria."

"Alexandria? Who is she?"

"My fiancée."

"Your fiancée?" WTF. You're engaged?" I tried to keep my voice down, but people had already heard us and began to stare.

"Melissa, calm down. You didn't think I would marry a nobody like you? You're a fuck—nothing more. You may be a high-priced whore, but you're still a whore." His eyes glazed over and his teeth gritted together as he delivered his speech about the type of woman I was and assessing my worth or lack thereof.

I grabbed my purse and left, crying the entire way home. Bryce was like every other asshole—they used people for their benefit. Even the first boy I slept with used me to help him pass his finals. Peyton used me for sex, and even though I didn't sleep with Bryce, that was always his intention.

Every man I wanted to give my heart to was a cheater. But was I any different? Every man I slept with was already in a relationship. I may not have known, but I still was the other woman. And truthfully speaking, my relationship with Bryce was more than as a friend. We may not have had sex, but we kissed each other like lovers. I had to classify myself in the same category as a cheater. That was the moment everything became clear: things needed to change.

I went home to my apartment that Peyton financed and contemplated my next move. I wanted to be free from this contract and tell Peyton the truth. I may have kissed Bryce, but I never slept with him. I hoped Peyton would be understanding. I knew Peyton would be pissed even if seemed as if he didn't want me anymore. Maybe we could agree to walk away from the contract with no penalties for either of us. If Peyton refused to release me from the contract with Infidelity, I would have to honor it for the next six months. But after that, I was done, and I refused to sell any more of my soul to anyone.

Once I was settled, I decided it was now or never. I needed to text him while my determination was strong. I feared that Peyton would wiggle his way back into my heart if I let him. I might have resented his treatment, but deep down I still cared for him.

ME: We need to talk.

Peyton: Monday. I'm not sure you will be able to speak with your mouth filled with my dick. I pay you to service my needs—not talk.

DICK. Why were all the men in my life assholes? I spent Saturday with my journal: I listed all of my decisions over the last few months and how I would do each one differently. Once I wrote almost every decision I'd made over the previous six months, I realized that everything was my fault. My dream became more important than living my life. My insecurities about never being good enough cost me more than I expected.

CHAPTER 14

The Betrayal

Melissa

Late Sunday afternoon, security called up to let me know my takeout had arrived, and the deliveryman was on his way up. I grabbed my wallet from the bedroom and headed for the door, just steps away when he knocked. I swung the door open and looked up into the blue abyss—eyes dark and cold.

"How the fuck did you get up here?"

He held up the bag of food. "I brought us dinner. Wasn't that nice of me?" Bryce sneered.

"You need to leave. Now," I demanded.

"Melissa, is that any way to thank me for thinking of you?"

"Bryce, you need to leave now, and don't come back."

He reached up with his free hand to pull a strand of red

hair into his fingers, and I backed up, which was a mistake. Bryce's tone was calm and playful, but his eyes were full of hate. The look reminded me of the other day when I tried to touch his necklace—only he looked deadlier today.

"Bryce, you need to leave before I call security."

Lord, I silently prayed, don't let him hear the panic in my voice.

I grabbed the door handle and tried to calmly shut the door. The key was already in the deadbolt, I just needed to close and lock. Three seconds tops and then I could call security and have him removed. Stepping away from the door, I tried to shut it, but it would budge. Bryce had slammed his hand over the door and held it open. I wasn't strong enough to push back.

Fear as I had never known surged through me as he pushed the door open and walked inside. My heart was a beating drum as my body trembled with fear, intensifying with each step as he came nearer. One step forward for him and one step backward for me, and then he stopped.

"Alexandria, I've missed you."

Alexandria? Did he really think I was his fiancée? "Bryce, listen to me. I'm not Alexandria. It's me. It's Melissa," I pleaded with him.

Seconds passed in silence, and he turned around, headed back for the door. I prayed he would leave, but I wasn't that lucky. With one hand he slammed the door shut and the other he turned the key in the deadbolt and removed it.

"You need to leave, Bryce!"

The key twisted between his fingers and flipped in the air as he turned toward me and slid the key into the front pocket of his jeans. Instinct took over; each step he took toward me, I took backward, step by step until I bumped into the Victorian chair at the edge of the area rug. A step to the right led me toward the couch; my legs stopped at the sofa with no escape. The farther I moved away from him, the redder his face turned. Eyes full of hate and rage, his lip curled up, and he bared his teeth. Bryce was gone and whoever just emerged showed no feeling.

"Alexandria, did you think I wouldn't know?"

"What? Bryce, I'm not Alexandria. Remember? It's Melissa."

"Shut up, whore."

I needed to buy time until I could find a way out or bring the Bryce I met at the club back from whoever this monster was. Bryce had the only key in his pocket, and I sure as fuck didn't want to get close. My phone was my only option, and it was under my books in the dining room. I just needed ten seconds to swipe Peyton's preprogrammed number on the keyboard—speed dial one. He might have been distant lately, but he wouldn't let someone hurt what was his—at least that was what I hoped.

Bryce continued to move closer, and I moved to the left on the far end of the sofa. From there, I'd have a straight shot to my phone. It would be my only chance to get past Bryce first. Slow motion took over as Bryce inched closer, and I moved closer to the back of the couch.

His fingers traced and tapped his lips. "I've been thinking... you never adequately thanked me for all the dinners and drinks."

"What?" This had to be a dream. This wasn't the sweet

man I'd met just a few weeks ago, the man who held me and made me want to tell him all my secrets.

"You owe me. I paid for a service—for you." His hand reached down and rubbed the front of his jeans. "I'm here to collect my money's worth."

"What?" My mind raced with what the fuck he was talking about; I never promised shit. He paid for our meal when we went out but… OMG—I told him about Peyton.

"Bryce, please. I'll pay you money, please," I begged. "How much do you want?"

He walked closer, and I made my run toward the table and freedom. Bryce had expected it and rushed over the couch, grabbed me by the arm, and pulled me closer. "I don't want money. I want this." His fingers burrowed into my crotch and his hands ran over my ass and up to my lips. "And this… and this."

"Please, Bryce. Don't! Just leave. I won't tell anyone you were here."

"Oh, Melissa, I don't care what you tell people. You're just an overpriced whore. I'm collecting a debt."

"Bryce, please."

"Well, since you begged so nicely." He let my arm go and took the key out of his pocket and headed toward the door. Relief only lasted a few seconds before he turned around and slapped me across the face. The force knocked me down, and my head slammed into the sofa table.

"Now, where would you like to pay your debt? On the floor like the dirty whore you are or in the comfort of your bed?"

He snatched my hair and dragged me into the bedroom and slammed me into the side of the dresser.

One glance at the bed and my heart stopped. The bungee cord Peyton used to secure me during sex stuck out from the mattress.

Fuck, please don't let him see it, please.

"Well. Well. Well. It looks like Miss Summers is a kinky whore, too," Bryce said as he bent down and pulled the cord.

Fuck, this wasn't good. I needed to get the hell out of there.

The bathroom.

I could lock myself in there until he left or Peyton arrived. But he could probably break the damn door down. I needed my phone to call for help. As he walked around the bed, he pulled the bungee cord, and the gleam sparkled in his eyes with even more excitement.

His focus never left me. I wasn't sure if I would have time, but I needed to try. I ran. Bryce jumped over the bed and had me by the hair before I even left the room.

As he pulled my back to his front, he rubbed his dick into my ass. "Do you feel that, Alexandria?"

My arms were held at my sides, but my legs were still free. I tried to kick, but he was much stronger than me.

"Fucking bitch, don't kick me."

He trapped my legs with his and twisted my body to face him. One of Bryce's hands reached around my neck and squeezed. Little black dots appeared in my vision as his hands squeezed tighter.

"Why. Can't. You. Just. Fucking. Listen?"

With each word, my body slammed into the wall, leaving me dazed.

"Oh, you like it rough, don't you, whore? Alexandria,

did you fuck all the college boys at Stanford or just the one?"

More pain shot through me as he slammed me against the wall a few more times before he released me. I dropped straight to the floor. Anger and disgust overtook him, causing his face to redden and his eyes to glaze. It was like he was possessed; his mind was in its own world—one minute I was Alexandria and the next Melissa. I wasn't sure if my life was in more danger as Melissa or as whoever this Alexandria was.

Pain radiated through my entire body; my head pounded and ribs ached from his abuse. His hands wrapped around my neck, smashing me into the wall one more time, and then he threw me on the bed. I tried to fight him, kick, or scratch him, but he overpowered me. Bryce had my hands secured in seconds and my feet within minutes. There was no escape for me tied down and him on top of me.

"Melissa, it time to play out your fantasy." He stood over me with the most sinister smile. "Well, I planned just to fuck you on the floor, but here you have everything already set up. Fuck me. I do know how to pick the perfect whores to fuck."

Tears clouded my vision. "Please, Bryce. Please, don't do this!" I screamed over and over, my voice hoarse from being strangled.

He carried on as if I wasn't even there. "Now, our safe word will be... hmm, let me think." Bryce looked up as if he was thinking and tapped his finger to his temple.

"Please stop. Please let me go," I pleaded. I needed to reach him, to bring Bryce back to the real world.

"You win—no safe word." He threw his head back and laughed.

Bryce's fingers dug into my thigh and then reached under my dress and pulled it up. "I like these." He traced my panties. "But they seem to be in the way." Bryce slid a finger under the seam and ripped them open to gain access to my most private area.

I twisted and turned, but restrained as I was, I didn't have much movement. Bryce gripped and squeezed my breast leaving a trail of pain. He climbed off me and unbuckled his belt, lowered his pants and boxers, and rubbed his hand over his dick. I wasn't sure who he thought I was. I just prayed he'd come to his senses before he hurt me anymore.

"Where would you like me to start—your pussy, ass, or mouth?" He reached down touching every spot he planned on invading.

"Bryce, please don't. Please just leave. I won't tell anyone," I begged over and over.

"There is nothing to tell. This is your rape fantasy. I'm just trying to make it as real for me as it is for you." A moan escaped as he gripped his dick and pulled. "Don't worry, I'll meet your needs, too. Isn't that what most women complain about?" He laughed.

"Please."

"Open your mouth. I need you to get me ready."

Ready? Fuck, he was already "ready." His hand ran up and down the length, waiting.

"Like what you see?" He stood proud of himself. "Don't worry; I'll fill every hole you have with my cum before the night is over." He laughed. "Maybe even twice if you're lucky."

Bryce climbed back on top of me and sat on my chest. "Open your mouth."

I sucked my lips into my mouth as a refusal. When I did, he placed his hand over my nose and cut off my oxygen until my mouth opened.

"Now, if you bite me, you'll regret it."

I closed my eyes and prayed for someone to help, but no one would. I was tied to a bed and locked in an apartment with a lunatic. He shoved his dick into my mouth repeatedly. He didn't care if I gagged. Tears flowed from my eyes as I gasped for breath, and my mouth filled with his cum.

"Drink it all up like a good girl. I'll let you rest until I am ready for the next hole." He walked out of the bedroom, and I heard him move around the other room.

Glasses clinked together. Fuck, he found the alcohol. I coughed and spit, ridding my mouth of his vile taste.

Bryce smiled as he walked back in a few minutes later, shot glass in hand. One look at me and he realized what I had done. Redness spread across his face, and he glared at me with hatred. "You fucking whore, I told you to swallow it, all of it."

He leaned down and picked up his belt. "Now I have to punish you." He wrapped the leather end in his hand as he swung the buckle against my bare skin over and over. Each time he smacked me, it caused his dick to jump with excitement.

Agony from the metal smashed across every inch of my

upper body, and angry red welts marked my skin as Bryce smirked in enjoyment.

I had two ways out of this nightmare: Peyton coming early or Bryce leaving soon, and neither seemed feasible. The thought that Bryce would be able to do whatever he wanted with me turned my stomach, but I was tied up with no way out. I didn't want to give up, but I also didn't want to live through any more of his torture. I only had one more option, to close my eyes and not wake up until it was over. I prayed darkness would take over before he used me up.

That wish wasn't granted.

I suffered for hours before the pain finally took over, and the world went black.

CHAPTER 15

Dreaded Dreams
Present

Melissa

Hours passed or maybe it had only been minutes since my humiliating examinations were over. I was placed in a private room and given a sedative. The new room was as cold and stale as the first one that showcased my shame. The only difference between now and the room with all the people was that now I was alone with no escape.

Shortly after the exam, the detective with the ugly brown suit left without a statement from me. He talked to the doctor and Peyton, but I was mute. He said he would be back later, but I didn't know what that meant. Later today? Tomorrow?

Hell, I didn't even know what day it was, much less the time.

I remembered the attack was before midnight Sunday, but I didn't know how long I lay on the floor before I was found or the amount of time I spent on that gurney stripped of all my dignity. None of that mattered as the sedative worked through my body. Darkness gradually overtook me, leaving my mind free to dream beautiful things. Unfortunately, the beauty soon turned into horrible images.

A path filled with flowers appeared before me. The sun shone on the horizon with perfect purple roses along the road. Birds sang in the trees hidden by branches full of leaves. I closed my eyes to inhale the fragrance, and when my eyes opened again, it was no longer filled with beauty. Now, the path where I walked was filled with pain and hurt.

"No, this isn't the path I chose. I picked the path on the right side. It was filled with love and joy. Take me back; I don't want to be on the left path filled with anger and hate," I screamed to no one. Hearing a response, I believed my screams must have been heard. I prayed or hoped that whomever was there was there to help me.

The voice was just above a whisper.

"You are not permitted on the other path. You must continue on the one you chose first." The cold and uncaring message echoed through the air.

"No! I want to be where the sun shines and flowers bloom," I screamed back as loud as I could. The voice had to listen. This way was filled with too much hurt and heartbreak. I wouldn't survive this path, and if I did, I'd be forever broken.

"You don't have a choice," he said. "You must finish this voyage first."

"But I can't. Please, it's too painful."

"I'm sorry. First complete this path, and then, and only then, will another path become available." While the words of the soft-spoken voice offered an apology, the tone was otherwise emotion-less and empty.

It wasn't sorry. This voice didn't care about the pain my choice caused.

I fell to my knees and begged for someone to listen and not leave me here. Silence was all I heard in return. Suddenly, a light flashed, and a new memory plowed into me. Pretty flowers and sunshine didn't fill this path. No, this journey would be dark and painful.

I was face down on the ceramic flooring. My body ached, as I vomited the contents of my stomach. I tried to remember how I ended up on the bathroom floor of the apartment where I'd lived for the last six months. My mind was confused as I tried to recall.

"I must've fallen on my way to the shower. No, I'd crawled here from the bedroom to take a shower. Why did I crawl?" The questions kept coming, but the answers were missing.

And then I heard the door open and I panicked.

Why, why was I scared?

I couldn't remember how I got on the bathroom floor and why I lay in a puddle of my vomit. I tried to move, but doing so caused more pain. And then a dreadful memory appeared.

My mind couldn't keep up with the constant flickers; every few minutes a new recollection flashed. Sunshine and then dark-ness before the sunshine recurred. It was like my brain fought between good and evil, but in the end, evil prevailed.

Colorful flowers turned into a broken body lying upon the floor. The sunshine was now a blond man with a devilish smile and a Southern drawl. The memories were there but confused; good and bad memories mixed with others. I wasn't sure if they were tied together or things I imagined. It was bits and pieces, like a jigsaw puzzle left undone, lying upon a table with only the border complete. The parts were all visible, but the middle pieces were scattered to the side. I was unsure if all the pieces were there or if some were missing.

"Miss Summers, I need to get your statement about what happened," a voice interrupted my memories.

I startled awake to find the detective from last night. He wasn't real. My mind was playing tricks to make me believe that the things I dreamed were real.

A minute or maybe an hour passed before I heard his harsh voice again. "Miss Summers."

Opening my eyes, I stared at the detective as he stood over me. His eyes were hollow, indifferent from all that he'd witnessed over the years. Hurt had a habit of destroying people from the inside out. Eyes were the windows to our souls, and the dullness of his told me that he'd seen more than his share of pain. Those experiences were slowly breaking him. That was my assessment, the one I chose to believe over the other option: he was just a coldhearted man who really didn't care.

"Miss Summers, you accused Bryce Spencer of rape, and I need you to tell me what happened. He was questioned last night by another detective." He stopped and waited for me to respond. When I didn't, he went on, "Miss Summer, Spencer and his attorney are at the station now to give a formal statement."

I didn't have the words to respond. I didn't want to remember, much less discuss it.

When I didn't respond, the detective continued, "Mr. Spencer tells a different story. He swore that the sexual contact was consensual. His attorney claims your accusation of rape is fraudulent." He leaned closer. "Mr. Spencer even alluded to the fact that you are a paid prostitute."

My eyes flew open. It wasn't a dream—it had happened. The nightmare and the memories were real. I swallowed any word lodged in my throat. My tears became my words, and my cries turned into my pleas to make it all stop.

"Get the fuck away from her. You. Are. Not. To. Talk. To. Her." The angry voice roared through the room, each word filled with rage, yet also protective and fierce like a dragon's fire defending a princess in a child's fairy tale.

"I filed a preliminary report," the detective said to Peyton, "based on *your* statement, but it won't mean shit if she doesn't talk. Bryce Spencer has a top attorney at his side and apparently more at his beck and call. I need more evidence to make this stick. As it is, by now Spencer's attorney is probably already filing counterclaims against Miss Summers for false accusations and defamation of character."

Both men stared at each other before the detective continued, "Have you ever heard of Alton Fitzgerald from Savannah?"

I looked from the detective to Peyton and back. I saw their expressions before they both turned to me. They didn't have to say the words. The silence told the entire story. I was fucked.

Finally, the detective broke the silence. "One of the

other detectives questioned Mr. Spencer. According to his statement, he claims the sex was entirely consensual."

He turned to me. "Claims it was you, Miss Summers, who begged him to play rough. He acknowledges having kinky sex with you, but swears you didn't have any of these injuries when he left."

I shook my head, wishing I could make it all go away.

But the detective didn't stop. "He believes the entire night was a ploy on your part to blackmail him." He turned and faced Peyton. "In fact, Mr. Harrison, don't you pay Miss Summers for sexual favors in return for her college tuition?"

Peyton had heard enough. "You fucking prick. Get the fuck out. Now!" His anger radiated throughout the room as his brown eyes turned black, and the vein in his temple pulsated.

I had only seen that look one time during the time we'd spent together. It was a look I'd never forget. I wasn't privy to what caused his foul mood, but I knew it had to do with a business meeting he had just come from. When he left that morning, he was fun and playful but when he returned he was short and irritable. He summoned me into the bedroom and used my body as his salvation.

I couldn't do it anymore. I'd listened to enough of the bullshit and posturing from the detective. He wasn't here to get my story, and his dead eyes weren't from the pain he'd witnessed. This man didn't care about my statement. He was here as a warning from Bryce and whomever the hell that Alton Fitzgerald man was. He was here to tell me that if I continued on this path—with my accusation—it would be one hell of a war.

My head pounded and stomach churned. I needed out of this world. Since leaving wasn't an option, I closed my eyes and prayed for my mind to be taken away to where love, peace, and equality ruled.

The sound of footsteps let me know that the two men were headed toward the door. Their conversation continued with heated words before the detective spoke louder. "Just remember..."

The rest of his sentence was cut off when the door clicked shut, and they both went into the hallway. Once again, I was alone in both the world and in my thoughts.

I don't know how much time passed. I hadn't heard the door open, yet I was no longer alone. A soft older voice broke through the fog. "Melissa, I brought something to help you sleep. Your friend said you were restless. This should help."

I just watched as the nurse injected a magic potion into my IV. Momentarily, I said a wish or maybe a prayer that she miscalculated the dose, giving me too much and freeing me—not only from the hospital but from the cold, cruel world.

A warm sensation traveled through my veins, filling me with a settling heat until it reached the part of my brain that shut out the world.

Maybe my wish had been granted, I thought, as I floated straight up to the skies. Higher and higher I went until I was close enough to touch the tip of a shooting star, but yet not close enough to grab it.

The medicine the kind nurse had injected took me on a ride through the land of rainbows and unicorns. It was magical, and I didn't want to leave, but then the colors disappeared, and I was back in the dark abyss, destined to relive the nightmare again and again.

Agony radiated throughout my body. Every part of me ached, the outer layer, from the cuts and bruises the doctor had described, to the inside, from pain so deep that only I knew it was there. My memory desperately tried to connect all the pieces of the puzzle that lay unfinished in my mind.

Pieces began to fit—the irregularly shaped corner snapped into the border of the puzzle. The next piece—flat and rounded on one side while zagged on the other—connected at a different angle. Slowly, each piece found its home until the puzzle of my mind had most of the pieces in place. There were a few holes that still needed to be worked out, but the picture was recognizable.

The reason I'd crawled to the bathroom for my shower slammed me harder than I'd expected. For a short time, I'd let myself believe that I'd fallen, but now with the puzzle almost complete, I knew that my reasoning was the furthest thing from the truth.

I'd wanted a hot, scalding shower to clean and disinfect my body from the horror.

The handsome blond man with that devilish smile was why I was dirty. He'd taken my body against my will and left it, as well as my heart and soul, broken. I didn't want to say the words that destroyed me, but I needed to accept the reality—Mr. Smiles had brutally raped me.

The memory continued to play. As I crawled on my hands and knees toward the bathroom doorway, the pain overpowered me, stopping my progression and my desire to be clean. The determination to rid my body of his nasty scent and disgusting semen gave me strength as my arms pulled me inch by inch into the bathroom. Yet I fell short when I collapsed just feet from the fresh, clean water.

Tears stung in my eyes with the realization that even if I'd managed to wash away his sins, nothing would erase the memory of that night and his touch. It was branded into my mind and embedded into my soul. That wicked moment would haunt my dreams or more accurately, my life for eternity.

From the bathroom floor, I'd heard the door alarm beep and panic surged through me, fearful of my attacker returning. My scrambled mind fought to focus on the voice I knew but couldn't remember.

"Melissa, where are you? Why was the front door unlocked and the alarm off?" His loafers tapped upon the hardwood floors as the man with the voice I knew walked deeper into the apartment.

I'd wanted to hide and protect myself from him finding me, but it was impossible. I didn't have the strength. I wasn't even able to crawl to the shower, and it was only a few feet away. Instead, I lay there as silently as possible, hoping he would leave, maybe assuming that I wasn't home.

During the last few hours all of my other wishes and requests had been ignored. I was certain that this one too would go unheard. Peyton would find me lying in my own vomit, covered in not only my blood but also my attacker's semen.

I tried to hide but there was nowhere to go. I didn't want to be seen like this—battered and used—but exhaustion had already won. I couldn't hide or move. I stayed upon the cold ceramic waiting to be found.

As the rest of the missing pieces came together, I realized my appearance didn't matter anymore. All the fancy clothes, money, and even Northwestern—none of it mattered. Every breath I took was one closer to how I felt. Dead.

His voice came nearer. "I left you a message last night. Why didn't you call me back? I'm pretty sure all of these little infractions are grounds for me to punish you."

I didn't answer. I couldn't.

The closer the footsteps came, vibrating through the apartment, the more irritated his voice grew. A few more steps before they came to a complete stop at the bedroom door. "Melissa, you must want a sore ass tonight. Where are you?"

I heard the buckle from his belt clink as he unfastened it.

Another couple of steps before Peyton found me. I could barely see him through my swollen eyes. When he stopped, his jaw tightened, and his belt fell to the floor, the buckle hitting the tile with a thud. The sounds that used to excite me now terrified me.

Time stood still.

His approach was in slow motion as his eyes wandered from the tip of my head to the tip of my feet. I knew by his expression that after tonight it wouldn't matter anymore. My life as I knew it was over.

Hands rushed to my face and pushed red strands of hair behind my ear. The anger in his voice overpowered the concern in his face. His voice was harsh and demanding when his eyes landed on me. "What the fucking hell happened?"

I tried to scoot away. His reaction scared me, reminding me of the man who'd attacked me. My recoil changed his features. All at once, his voice became soft and calm even though his eyes still held fire—red-hot sparks ignited when he saw the damage to my body.

"Melissa, my beautiful girl, what happened? Talk to me.

Please. Who hurt you?" His hands stroked my face and wiped the tears.

My throat burned, and my words strained. "Please don't tell my parents. Please."

"Okay, whatever you want. Just tell me who hurt you."

"Please. I need a shower. Please..." My eyes finished what my words couldn't as more tears pooled with the others.

"Sweetheart, I'm sorry. You can't shower. You need to go to the hospital."

"No," I protested. "I can't. No. People will find out what happened. Please." Even though my words weren't above a whisper, it was as though I'd screamed them from the highest mountain.

A steady hand brushed against my cheek.

"Melissa, sweet girl, you can't shower." His voice hitched. "I need you to trust me. You need a hospital. You're hurt."

"People," I cried. "T-they'll know."

"Know what?"

"Know about our..." I refused to finish the sentence, to admit what I'd become.

"Sweetheart." His hand brushed away my tears. "I'll handle it. Just don't say anything to anyone. Let me do all of the talking. Trust me."

I didn't have another choice. He was right: I needed help, lying broken on the bathroom floor. Without Peyton's help, I would die in my vomit. I had to believe that for now he would protect me. I also I knew that once I revealed the truth of my attack, he'd discard me like yesterday's news. I'd made a series of misjudgments. As I accepted his help, I prayed that trusting him wasn't another one.

Strong hands wrapped around my body, picking me up and

carrying me to the bed. Next, he sheathed me in a blanket. As I was again raised off the bed and placed against his broad chest, my body felt lighter.

"Sweetheart, I don't need all the details now, but I need you to tell me who hurt you."

I was too tired and exhausted to lie. "His name is Bryce Spencer."

The words were barely murmurs, but with the way the gentleness in his eyes was replaced with rage and his arms held me tighter, I knew he heard me.

"Melissa." His tone was calm and yet stern. "Remember, our agreement is private. You are not to discuss it. You are nothing more than a family friend. Nothing else. Do you understand?"

His words punctuated with a soft kiss on my forehead were the last things I remembered as his scent engulfed me.

CHAPTER 16

A Message

Melissa

"Stop!" I screamed. "No! Get off me!"
"Oh baby, you like it. Don't you? Playing hard
to get?"
"Get off me!"
"Don't worry...rape fantasy...."
"Please. I'm begging."
Jolted awake from my nightmare, I was shaking uncontrollably as pain radiated through my body, and nausea
took over. My stomach twisted and turned, vomit lodged
in my throat, threatening to be purged. My body lunged
forward as at the same time a small basin was placed in
front of me. My head throbbed and throat burned from the
acidic bile.

My head remained over the basin until the bile ran dry,

and the dry heaves subsided. A hand upon my shoulder eased me back toward the bed until my head hit the pillow. Looking up, I recognized her. She was one of the nurses from the night before, or was it the day before?

I still had no concept of time. It all blended into before or after the rape.

The nurse placed a white cloth around the back of my neck and wiped my face with another piece of fabric. Though her actions were caring, her smile appeared indifferent. Her eyes seemed cold and filled with uncertainty—like she was waiting for something. To an observer, her words and gestures would appear tender; however, her death glare toward me told a different story. It was as if she knew something that I didn't, and she was patiently waiting for an opportunity to strike.

"I need to make a call," Peyton said, his voice tight yet controlled.

My view of him had been blocked until he stood up. His six-foot-four body towered over the nurse. Worry lines and dark circles marred his eyes. His hair was wild from all the times he ran his fingers through it. Peyton didn't have many quirks, but he had the habit of pulling his hair when he was troubled. I wasn't sure if his concern was about the possibility of our arrangement being revealed or my injuries. As he stepped closer to the bed, it was obvious that the caring man from last night was gone, replaced with a stolid demeanor.

"My secretary is bringing some clothes for you." When our eyes locked, I heard the words he didn't speak: *"You will regret it if you open your mouth."* I didn't respond, the guilt of my betrayal forefront in my mind.

Turning away from me, he nodded to the nurse.

The callousness in his words and movements told me that he too had a secret but like the nurse was unwilling to share.

I glanced at the door as he left and returned my sights to the nurse. She waited, but once the click of Peyton's shoes disappeared, her eyes drifted back to me. Time once again stopped as she measured me and contemplated her words. Planting a broad smile on her face as if she were there as a friend to cheer me up, the nurse lowered her voice, her tone sounded caring, but the words were nothing but vile and hateful. She was there to put the final nail in the casket and send me straight to hell.

"You are nothing more than a lying whore who gets paid for sex. Everyone will know the truth soon enough. If you think you can accuse Bryce Spencer of rape, you'd better think again. No one will believe you, especially the police."

I don't know what shocked me more—her words or her hatred toward me. I was in disbelief; she was supposed to be there to help not blame me.

She hesitated for a minute and looked in the direction of the door before she started speaking again. "Bryce is a good man and comes from a good family. You're nothing more than a gold-digging whore who is after his money. I saw you at the club flirting—begging for something. When I overheard what your pimp told the police, I called Bryce. He told me all about your arrangement." She stopped for a moment before her detestation continued, "Bryce would never hurt anyone. He doesn't need to rape..." She laughed to herself as if what she said was funny. "...there are plenty of us who willingly give Bryce what he wants, and we all know what he likes. He likes to have fun." She took another breath, ready to strike another blow, but the door creaked open. Her voice lowered to a mere whisper. "You just don't want him..." She nodded toward the person entering. "...to know that you're nothing more than a lying whore, trying to get money and protect yourself."

I didn't want anything from Bryce. I knew he had money by the way he carried himself, but I wasn't interested in that. I'd already had someone with money who'd discarded me. I had just wanted someone to treat me like I mattered. I didn't want to be a fuck toy anymore. I'd wanted an untainted companionship with no financial obligations.

The nurse planted a giant smile on her face, turned, and continued speaking to me. "I'll be back in a little while to check on you and..." She turned back to me, leaned in, and pretended to check the IV line as she delivered her final attack. "I know you're a liar, and soon the world will know when your name is accidentally released..."

I closed my eyes as memories flooded my mind, and my body ached. I needed to escape—to find a place to hide—even if it was only mentally. I didn't want to listen to or be touched by anyone. The thought of people looking at me made me even sicker. Not just because I was beaten and bruised, but because I was ashamed, humiliated, and now threatened.

All of the decisions of the last few months were the reasons why I was lying in a hospital bed shattered. I could blame Peyton's indifference for my search for companionship. I could blame Bryce for abusing me, but the truth was simple. I was here because of me.

Needing an escape, I searched for the clock, but the one from before was gone, replaced with one less friendly. This one's arms sat on the ten and two, mocking my pain with a smile that screamed 'I told you so.' Though the second hand ticked away minutes, it never allowed me a moment of freedom, refusing my request for happy memories. The hands continued to move as if it were just another hour, minute, or second, those without worries.

Each tick of this clock reminded me of the choices I'd made and the mistakes that had left me numb. I wanted to forget the memories, but the cruel clock continued its tick-tock, demanding that I accept my punishment. This time it wasn't to be fun or sexy. The punishment the clock demanded was to remember and relive all the pain.

Once again, my choices had been taken away by others based on one wrong decision and one wrong turn in the road. Now, even objects that should have no say in my life controlled my thoughts with a simple tick.

I was determined to be lost in another time. I begged and begged the new clock to allow me access until finally, it surrendered, and I prevailed. As I hid behind the invisible shield, my world was again happy until it wasn't.

A loud voice cracked my shield just enough for sounds to penetrate my world, but the actual words were missing. The content of the phrase was repeated but it was distant and unclear. More sounds invaded my space like a pounding against a door. Though I tried to ignore the intrusion, the crack was too much to repair.

I was between worlds—my body was physically in the

room, as my mind wandered to the other—until one final blow to the tear brought the door down. I was back from my escape.

"Melissa, we need to talk," Peyton said.

"What?"

I was confused. I remembered the nurse had left the room after Peyton came back, but I couldn't recall how long ago that had been. Flashes of my search for my clock, my friend who previously saved me, were a blur. I recalled the argument I'd had with the new clock, begging it to shelter me, but I couldn't remember when it finally accepted me into its world—I just knew it had.

Now I was back.

"How are you feeling?" Peyton asked with annoyance in his tone.

I didn't answer. Instead, I turned away to face the window.

He had taken away my solace, pulled me away from the clock's protection. I didn't want to talk to anyone—especially now that I knew Bryce had people everywhere, people who would remind me that I was nothing more than a paid whore and who threatened to expose me to the press for the world to see. In their eyes, whores didn't have many rights, even fewer than those granted by the men who used and abused those whores.

"Melissa! I asked you a question. Fucking answer me. How are you feeling?"

"I feel like fucking peaches and cream." The venom in my voice spoke louder than my actual words. Tears dripped down my face as Peyton reached out to pull me closer. I pulled away as panic overtook all reasoning. "Get off me! Please just get off me."

He stepped back. Anger took over and his eyes bore into mine. The truth was clear: even broken I was still his until I wasn't anymore. I'd signed the agreement. My choice was gone. I had to listen to and obey him. Peyton controlled me. He owned me until he decided our agreement was done, which would probably be sooner rather than later. Once he discovered that this rape wasn't a random act, that I'd accepted a date from my attacker, any and all compassion would be gone.

I looked up and met the eyes of the man who promised to help me achieve my dreams. He was the same man who'd also betrayed my trust when he turned me into his whore and hid our treachery for his pleasure and my greed.

I'd broken the rule when I'd told Bryce about our agreement. No one was supposed to know about the agreement —especially family or friends. It was another decision I regretted among many. Bryce had taken that information as an invitation to use my body as he wanted. He paid for a service when he paid for lunch, and it was his right to collect. In his mind, he could do whatever he wanted to me, and the sad part was that he knew that when he did, no one would care.

At one time, I'd been too naive to understand that money and power ruled in this world. Not anymore. Now I knew. Those elements would always prevail, and I didn't have either.

Peyton stared down at me with no emotion. "I have learned a few things since I found you." He took a breath.

"This..." He swirled his hands around the room. "...wasn't rape."

"What the fuck? You saw me." Pain permeated my voice. "You know—"

Once again, he interrupted me. "Shut the fuck up and listen. You weren't attacked. You invited him in. If I would have known that when I found you, I would have left you there."

"Peyton..." The pain he'd caused with his indifference months ago didn't even come close to what he was delivering now. My stomach turned as vomit once again threatened. The cold was back, making my hands shake and my body shiver.

Once again, I was completely shattered.

"Now, may we continue?" He didn't give me a chance to answer. "This is what the police have been told. I allowed you to live in my apartment because your mother and my wife are best friends. We never told your parents of those arrangements because you were afraid they would be hurt that they couldn't provide for their only daughter."

He stood in front of my bed and waited for an answer or acknowledgment that I understood. When I didn't respond, he bent down, his face inches from mine. "Do. You. Understand?"

I nodded.

Peyton hesitated for a few moments. "I've already talked to Detective March and informed him that I jumped to conclusions when I found you, but now, since you've confessed your whorish ways, I explained that you invited Bryce into my apartment to apparently satisfy your *rape fantasy.*"

"That's a lie. You know it. W-why? Why would you lie?" Hatred and pain radiated from my body and voice.

"I have the call log from your phone. I know about the club and the lunches. I know everything." The coldness of his voice sent a chill running up my spine.

I knew Peyton could destroy me if I didn't follow his instructions. I shook my head, refusing to cry another tear in front of this asshole. I wouldn't give him the satisfaction.

"Finally," he said, "Infidelity doesn't exist, and neither does our contract. If you are smart, you'll forget they exist."

He turned away and walked out the door without even a goodbye. He'd made his decision. Our contract was over and so was his concern for me.

CHAPTER 17

Dismissed

Melissa

The time came for me to leave the hospital and take care of myself—by myself. My forced seclusion was another emotional violation as I relived not only the abuse in my head but also the betrayal of being thrown away like trash. Though the memory of the rape was torturous, it was the memories of all the happy times over the last six months that crippled me. Even the months with the fewer visits haunted me. I didn't know saying three little words would send Peyton running, but *'I love you'* was like a light switch. They flipped from on to off, and our time together just vanished. The weekly visits that once went on for days became monthly visits that lasted hours and the calls, texts, and playful messages disappeared.

The rape created much of the same reaction in Peyton.

The night he found me, he'd been comforting and caring, the next day distant. By the time I was released, he'd disappeared with a single text.

PEYTON: **Car will pick you up and take you back to the apartment.**

I FIGURED out quickly that the road map of my life had taken a detour, and the new road would be hard terrain. The fact that a set of clothes had been left at the nurse's station with my name said everything. In the real world, it shouldn't have mattered. I'd said no, but we didn't exist in the real world. In the entitled world where it happened, I betrayed him by inviting Bryce into my life. My unwillingness was irrelevant.

My life had become an emotional rollercoaster. It had significant downward dips and only rose in little hurdles, before falling back toward the ground. Physically my body began to heal, but emotionally the pain bubbled deep under violet bruises that lingered as their color changed.

I refused the prescription for pain medication when I left the hospital. The physical pain couldn't even compare to how I struggled emotionally. Instead of making it go away, I used the pain as a reminder of all the hurt and anger I felt. The pain was my source of empowerment. The more the anger grew, the more determined I became to fight back. I wanted to punish Bryce Spencer, but the fear of Peyton and Infidelity made me hesitate.

As my fingers mindlessly traced the letters, over and

over, of each word written in that damn cruel letter the limo driver had handed me, my mind replayed the scene of my dismissal.

The car owned by Infidelity came to a stop in front of the apartment building. As I got out, the driver handed me an envelope. "Don't open it until you are in the apartment," he said with a quick nod as he then shut the back door, turned away, opened the driver's door, and disappeared.

Six months ago, I'd been catered to and pampered, but those days were over. It seemed that even the 'help' was now dismissing me like I was nothing—a penny dropped on the road but not worthy enough to be picked up.

As I entered the building, the vibrant world where I'd arrived six months ago no longer existed. The security guard was away from his desk, and the doorman was on break. No other residents wandered through the lobby—it was a ghost town. I wasn't sure how they'd done it, but the message was clear: I was no longer welcome here. I was invisible, nothing more than a figment of their imagination.

The elevator doors opened as if waiting for my arrival. I stepped in and the doors closed behind me. I rode alone up to the apartment. Once the elevator reached the seventh floor, the doors opened, and I faced the entrance to hell.

I didn't want to be there. I wanted the doors to close and take me back down. But the doors stayed open and waited for me to exit. The envelope with my name scrolled across the front that the driver had given me was similar to the one I'd first seen on the front seat of my car nearly a year ago.

I recognized the writing, and it didn't take a genius to figure out that it wasn't a love letter. It was my dismissal. The letter along with the fact that no one had visited me since the detec-

tive left led me to believe the fate of my future had been decided.

The driver had told me to wait until I was in the apartment to read it, but I was sick of following orders. Determined to regain some control, I ripped that fucking envelope open right at the doorway while still in the hallway.

Who would stop me? I'd become a ghost that no one saw. My hands shook as I read.

MISS SUMMERS,

As of June 1, 2015, your services for employment are no longer required, and future compensation has been suspended permanently. Any past payment is under review for violation of the agreement and may be eligible for reimbursement.

Please note, the scholarship to Northwestern University was contingent upon your continued employment with our company. Therefore, it is with great regret that Northwestern has rescinded your scholarship. You have been placed on academic suspension until further notice, effective immediately.

You are also required to move out of the provided housing within 30 days from the date of your dismissal. Please be aware other penalties could be assessed against you. We are sorry for your misfortune; however, a breach of the contract cannot be tolerated under any circumstances.

Per your contract, you are required to meet with one of our executives for a formal interview. Once the exit interview is complete, you will be informed if our client wishes to invoke any other penalties for your breach of contract.

Sincerely,

Karen Flores

I READ the letter multiple times, each pass-through a little quieter in my head and slower in hopes the letter would fade away just as my voice had. In reality, the more I read it, the more it became real. I repeated the words until they were a soundtrack of the scrolled letters blasting in my head.

I don't know how long I sat in tears in front of the doorway to hell, but the minute I entered the apartment something changed. My eyes were dry, my soul drained, and my heart was as hard as stone.

For some reason, I recalled the children's game that kids often played to determine who would go first—rock, paper, scissors. The rock broke scissors. Paper covered rock. And scissors cut paper. Independently, each had the strength to beat the other, but together they were unstoppable.

My heart was the rock, my knowledge was the paper, and by God, in that moment I became determined that I would be the scissors. Knowledge was my gift. My broken heart was my determination, and every motherfucking person who'd hurt me was my strength. The scissors would cut, the paper would reveal, and the rock would break each one of them. I made myself a promise: they would all bleed by my hand. It may not be today but it will happen someday.

As I looked around the empty apartment, I felt the change in the atmosphere—cold and unwelcoming. It held an odor of superiority and entitlement, not the sexy citrusy scent from the past. Even the sweet scent of a lavender candle couldn't mask the foul smell. The eeriness shook me to the core.

The apartment appeared the same as the day I'd moved in. Everything had been cleaned. No one who walked in now would believe that a violent rape had taken place within these walls only days before.

Memories of the horrid night flashed before my eyes day and night. It didn't matter if I was awake or asleep: all I saw were the faces of all the ones who hurt me. It wasn't just Bryce's face but also the face of the man who left me when I needed someone the most. I'd needed and craved comfort, but all I'd received was a dismissal. I was now alone with an eviction notice. However, I didn't need to leave yet. I had one month to fester in my poor decisions and nurture the vengeful bitch who was coming to life within me.

I wasn't the only one who would pay the debt of lies and deceit. No matter the cost, others also had overdue payments to make—and they would, as long as I had anything to say about it.

I'd wanted Bryce to pay for his sins but the constant reminders of my agreement gave me doubts in the pursuit of justice. The question was no longer if Bryce would pay, but how he would pay.

I also had an internal battle brewing within me, questioning who else would be punished and who would be indebted for my suffering. Bryce had stolen a piece of me when he refused to stop when I begged. However, he wasn't the only one who took from me. Others confiscated something even more precious than my body: they'd taken my soul.

Just as the nurse from the hospital hammered the final nail into the casket that held my mental peace, the letter from Infidelity drove the final nail into my heart.

Emotionally, I was dead, and revenge would be served to those who stole my life from me.

CHAPTER 18

Truth or Justice

Melissa

I sat alone in the apartment for two days before I finally picked up the phone and called someone for help. I tried to be strong and believe in all the words I'd said to myself only days before, but the truth was that I was too exhausted to fight. My body hurt, and my mind constantly replayed the rape. I knew that I wouldn't be able to battle the demons by myself anymore. I needed help to heal, and there was only one person who had always been there for me: my mother.

"Mom, I need you," I cried into the phone for help.

"Melissa, what's wrong, honey?" Her voice was soft.

"Please. I need you to come here."

"Okay, honey. I'll be there as soon as I can. Please, tell

me what's wrong." The panic in her voice rushed through the phone.

"I can't. Please don't hate me." That was the last thing I said as I hung up the phone. I knew that my mother would worry and fear the worst, but I didn't have the words. She called repeatedly, but I wouldn't answer. I couldn't tell her on the phone what had happened.

What would I say? "Mom, I was raped, and your best friend's husband paid me for sex."

My mother and father arrived in less than twenty-four hours after my call. She'd packed their bags, and then they drove the fifteen hours straight from Myrtle Beach to Evanston. I knew they would have questions about the apartment and why I wasn't in a dorm like I'd told them. I wasn't able or willing to talk about it. I just needed my mother to comfort me.

From the time she arrived, my mother held me and let me cry, never questioning what had happened. Bruises and marks were still visible all over my body. She had to know, but allowed me the opportunity to cope without demanding answers.

My father tried his best to be patient, but he wanted and needed to know who hurt his daughter. He pushed for details—he wanted someone punished. I wasn't able or ready to open up to anyone. It would be hard enough to tell my mother. How does one tell her father she was raped? It was my mother who convinced my father to head back to Myrtle Beach. She knew it would be easier for me if we were alone.

Peyton became the hero when my mother learned how much he'd helped me over the months. He added insult to injury when he stopped by the apartment to offer us the use of his private plane to return us home instead of flying commercial. But it was all an act. He was a chameleon. The minute my mother left the room, his fury rained down on me. He reached over and squeezed my upper arm, pulling me closer. "Melissa, if they find out the truth about us, you'll regret it."

"You're hurting me."

"Sweetheart, you haven't felt hurt yet." Though his voice was low, the heat of his breath was on my ear. "Remember what I said. I pulled some strings. Your rape report and the evidence they collected have been destroyed. As far as the police are concerned, you had a misunderstanding with Spencer. Sex games. Do. You. Understand?"

"Yes." My resolve to not let him see more of my emotion dissolved as tears fell.

Peyton pulled me into his embrace as my mother walked back into the room. "Everything will be okay, Melissa. You can come back to work at Harrison." He patted me on the back. His last words were under his breath. "Never step foot in my company again, or you will regret it."

"Peyton," my mother said. "I can't thank you enough for everything." She came closer and hugged him.

I stared in disbelief as he fucking smiled at her and patted my arm where only moments before he'd had it in a death grip. It made me sick how quickly and easily he'd lied, not to mention the way my mother fawned over his kindness. It wasn't my mother's fault she praised him so much. Hell, I'd been the one who'd told her the damn lie in the first place.

Once Peyton left, I fell into my mother's arms and bared my soul, telling her everything that had happened with Bryce, everything except his name. She listened and never judged or criticized me for any of my actions. Of course, she only knew half the story. I couldn't risk any more than I'd already lost.

Though, I still wanted Bryce to pay for what he did, I hoped if I walked away quietly, Peyton and Infidelity wouldn't pursue me. It was my only comfort in the nightmare.

We flew home the following week. When I packed, I left one item in the apartment that I'd brought—the key necklace. I didn't want any memories of this fucking place or of Peyton.

From the time we arrived home, my father never stopped badgering me. His insistence to contact the police never ended, but I refused. He wanted both legal and monetary compensation for me. The person who hurt me needed to be brought to justice and the apartment building needed to pay financially for lack of security.

"Melissa, you deserve for someone to be punished. If we sue that damn apartment complex for your being hurt, you could go to any college you want," my father bellowed at me.

Damn, didn't he think I wanted justice for what happened to me? I was scared. I had to worry about more than Bryce. I also had Infidelity and Peyton hanging over my head. I lived in fear, thinking of all of the Infidelity rules that I'd broken. Recalling the dismissal letter, the possible penalties they could enforce against me kept me up most nights.

Over a month had passed since I had arrived home, and no one had contacted me. The nightmares of the rape were regular—every night and often all-night long. The only positive thing was that Peyton no longer haunted me. He had moved on with his life and left me alone. I kept close tabs on Bryce through tabloids. He had gone back to Savannah and the life that waited for him. It made me sick every time his image was captured in the paper, smiling and happy.

Fuck, even though I still wanted that bastard to pay, I'd begun to believe that as long as I kept my mouth shut, I would be safe. Besides, revenge was best served cold. Isn't that the saying?

I'd spent too much time alone, replaying the last six months in my head. I needed to move on and live my life. To that end, I decided to sign up for online classes for the fall semester. Business no longer interested me. I wanted to do something that would allow me to help other people. At first, I decided upon nursing school. And then I changed my mind, deciding to help other abused women, possibly as a counselor.

Perhaps Bryce's fan-club bitch nurse was one of the reasons I changed from my original major of business and into a profession that helped people. I just hoped that one day she and karma would have a nice get-together that included Bryce.

"Melissa, you have mail," my mother said as she walked back toward my room and knocked on the open door. "How was today?"

"Better." I smiled at her.

She handed me the letter. "There's no return address."

My brow arched, and panic soared through me as my mother turned to walk away.

"Mom, please stay."

She nodded and took my hand.

I flipped it over. It was just a plain white envelope typed with my name and address. I pulled the flap open and found a newspaper clipping folded in half, and a sticky note was attached to the inside.

MELISSA,
   Call Tim at 312-xxx-xxxx

I PULLED off the sticky note and read the headline.

"*ANOTHER RAPE COVER-UP or Was it a Hoax?*"

A COLD SHIVER shook my body and a coating of sweat covered my skin as I scanned the article. Who the hell knew about this, and who the hell would want it public?

The answer to the second question was no one. So who had opened the Pandora's box? The article detailed all of my injuries, dates of the incident, and even a copy of my medical report with my name blacked out. The first line was in bold.

EDWARD BRYCE SPENCER OF SAVANNAH, *Georgia, was accused*

of raping an eighteen-year-old student of Northwestern University in Evanston, Illinois. Mr. Spencer denied the claim, stating that the act was consensual. After the incident and the initial charge, the student disappeared and hasn't reported back to Northwestern. An Internet search has found this student back in her hometown of Myrtle Beach, South Carolina. Another cover-up? Why were the charges never filed, and where did the initial report go?

THE ARTICLE DIDN'T END THERE. It included the location of the alleged rape, including the address, and listed Peyton Harrison as the leaseholder.

Terror surged through me, my body falling to the floor as I wrapped my arms around myself. Lying in the fetal position, I closed my eyes and rocked, praying it would all go away.

"Melissa! Melissa! Oh my God, what's wrong?" My mother's voice rose each time she called my name, and yet each time she was more distant as I entered my own world.

Screams I didn't even recognize erupted from inside me as fear pushed me back into the past. Time stopped, and I was transported back into Peyton's bedroom with Bryce on top of me. All of the pain and memories flashed back until I saw only black.

"Melissa, darling, are you awake?" my mother asked as she lay on my bed next to me, her arms tightly wrapped around my waist.

"Yeah, Mom, please tell me it was a dream. I can't relive it again. I can't." I rolled into my mother's embrace for comfort.

"Darling, I wish I could, but I can't." She lifted my chin so that our eyes would meet and smiled. Sitting up, my mother reached for my hairbrush on the nightstand and softly pulled it through my hair as she did when I was a little girl. She combed through it and held me and let me cry until sleep overtook me.

The sun was shining through my window as voices rang from the other room, waking me from my rest. "Why would you release the report to the press? Melissa was just starting to live her life again." My mother sounded angry. Though her voice was low, every word held contempt.

"Someone needed to pay," my father replied. "Fuck, Maggie. Melissa won't go to the police. At least this way someone is held accountable. These people have millions, and the only thing they understand is money."

"How did you even find out the name?"

"Maggie," Regina's voice said, "someone needs to be punished."

"Keep your voice down. Melissa finally fell asleep."

My angry mother seemed to be the only person who cared more about me than fucking justice or money.

I couldn't take anymore. The little bit I'd overheard told me enough.

My father was responsible for the news release. He was the one who'd opened a Pandora's box. I grabbed my phone, car keys, and the article that was on my dresser and went out the back door before anyone would see me. I drove to the same spot on the beach where I had sat the night of my graduation dinner.

The air was warm, and the sun shone down on the sand filled with people. As many people that were here, the beach was still somewhere I could be alone. I debated in my head what I needed to do next. Calls to Peyton and Infidelity were at the top of the list. I needed to forewarn them of the fallout. It wasn't like I owed them loyalty. I considered it more of a preemptive strike. I also wondered if I should call the guy from the sticky note and explain that the incident was a misunderstanding—as Peyton had called it—but my stomach clenched and twisted with that lie.

I didn't want this circus. I also refused to ruin any more of my life or reputation. My father had opened the Pandora's box. He thought it contained the answer to justice. It didn't. It held my life, and now once again, it was in shambles.

When I reached for my phone, the one I'd silenced, I saw the screen. I had nine missed phone calls. Hell, on a typical day, I wouldn't have any calls at all. I scrolled the numbers—five missed calls were from my mother. I'd gone to the beach because I didn't want to talk to anyone—not even her. And then I thought about just sending her a text, but after all she'd done for me, she deserved a call to let her know that I was okay and just needed some time to be alone.

Three of the numbers were from Illinois, and one was unknown. I listened to the voicemails left.

DETECTIVE MARCH: "**Miss Summers, I need you to call me.**"

Detective March: "**Miss Summers, please call. It is urgent that you return my call.**"

Detective March: "Miss Summers. If I do not hear from you, a subpoena will be issued for you to return to Evanston to give a formal statement."

THE LAST MESSAGE was from someone else.

BRYCE: "You fucking whore. Do you think that you or your white-trash family can ruin my life with blackmail? I will destroy you."

CHAPTER 19

Running

Melissa

"Tell us what happened, Miss Summers."

I sat in an interview room of the Evanston police department. My mother, father, and Regina waited in another place as I answered questions about the night Bryce attacked me. The detective was serious when he said they would issue a subpoena for me to return to Evanston. I was served just days after his call and was required to be back the following week.

The article that was printed in the paper made the department and Detective March look incompetent, and they were none too happy. The release of my rape report made it appear that special favors were doled out and possible compensation paid to look the other way.

"Where did you meet Bryce?" Detective March had been badgering me for an hour.

The questions came fast but my answers were slow. It wasn't that I didn't remember. I didn't want to remember, and I also didn't want to involve Infidelity nor Peyton in this mess. They deserved to be, but what would it accomplish now? Nothing but more problems for me. I shook my head and repeated the same answer for the fifth time. "Bryce approached me and invited me upstairs at the club *Final Stand.*"

"Why are you claiming rape now when you said back in May that it wasn't rape. I think your words were that it was a misunderstanding." Sarcasm dripped from his voice.

Rage poured through me. "I never said shit to you. I believe it was Peyton Harrison who informed you that my rape was a 'misunderstanding.'" I used my fingers as quotation marks to prove my point. "No one asked me fucking shit! No one followed up with me! No one!"

"Miss Summers, I came to your hospital room and tried to talk to you, if you remember." His voice raised a notch, but it was the tone that gave away his mood—pissed. "You refused to talk."

"I was in fucking shock." Defeated. That's how I felt. I played my words over on what I just said. Peyton Harrison... Fuck! Damn! I leaned back and took a deep breath. I just brought Peyton into this shit. Detective March tried to provoke me to make me slip up. I was just where he wanted me—in quicksand and sinking fast.

"Oh, yes. You mentioned Peyton Harrison." He stopped and flipped papers over one at a time to delay until he found the one he wanted. "Let's review what I know, shall we. In May, you were brought to the hospital beaten. Mr. Harrison claimed Bryce Spencer broke into his apartment and brutally raped you. Demanded we arrest him." He leaned down and got right in my face. "Does that sound familiar?" He waited, and when I didn't respond, he continued. "Based on those claims, my partner interviewed Mr. Spencer, and do you know what he said?"

"Stop, please stop," I cried out. "He did rape me! I was too scared to come forward. I would have..." I realized what I was about to say and stopped.

"You would have... Would you like to finish that statement?" He paused and waited. "No? Then I'll continue with my story. According to Mr. Spencer, you invited him up for dinner—in fact, he brought dinner for you, didn't he?"

"I didn't invite him. He just showed up!" Why did someone have to drag this shit up again? I just started to live again. I wanted to fucking kill my father and Regina for their help in getting justice for me.

"Miss Summers. He just happened to know you ordered takeout. Didn't you call security and tell them you were expecting a visitor?"

"No! I told them I ordered takeout!"

"And Mr. Spencer just happened to show up with dinner after you informed security you would have a delivery? Convenient." He fucking smirked. He wasn't done and was about to go in for the kill.

"Stop! Stop!" Tears fell fast on my shirt.

"Mr. Spencer admits the two of you engaged in kinky but..." He extended the word *but*. "...consensual sex. He believes your invitation that night was a scam to extort money from him."

The room was silent except for my crying. I tried to process all the things that the detective said, and it all came together. Bryce was right—they would never believe me.

"Would you like to know what my captain thinks?" he asked mockingly.

"No! It's not true. You really think I wanted to be beaten and raped repeatedly?" It was now a screaming match for us.

March waited until the room fell quiet again and nodded his head toward the window. "My captain, he thinks you invited Mr. Spencer up and seduced him to play out your fantasy. When Mr. Spencer left, you had an accomplice help stage your rape claim in order to collect money."

"I never asked for a fucking dime—I didn't want anything from him. Not his fucking money and I sure as hell didn't want him to shove his dick inside of me!" Anger took over, allowing me to find the voice I needed to project the injustice of his words. My words were loud and full of spite; I was positive the entire building heard me screaming at Detective March.

Bam.

The solid wood door slammed against the wall and chairs scattered as my mother rushed in to protect me.

"Leave her alone." Warm arms wrapped around my back and pulled me into her embrace. My father and Regina stood a short distance from her. My mother's protectiveness only fueled the detective's determination to pull me into the sinkhole he found himself in after the newspaper's report.

Fuck. Why didn't my father just let it go? Justice. The

blank look on my face answered March's question. His eyes sparkled, and he went in for the kill.

"Miss Summers, isn't it true that you actually have a financial agreement with Peyton Harrison?" He waited for my answer. "You were paid a large sum of money and in addition, he supplied you with a scholarship to Northwestern, a luxury apartment, and monthly deposits into your account..." He let his words drag. "... and in return you fulfilled his kinky sexual fantasies." A loud gasp filled the room as he went on. He looked up and locked eyes with Regina. "Mrs. Harrison, are you married to Peyton Harrison?"

"What the fuck is he talking about, Melissa?" Regina's high heels echoed off the floor.

I sank deeper into my mother's chest, hysterical. My mother released her arms and pulled my face to hers. "Peyton and you? Is what he is saying true?"

I tried to divert my eyes away. Unfortunately, they fell on my angry father. "You sold yourself like a common whore?"

March pushed on. "In others words, a prostitute for Mr. Harrison."

Detective March knew what he was doing—divide and conquer.

All eyes locked on me and their look of pity when we arrived transformed into looks of disgust. I did what I had always done when upset: I ran. Pushing out of my mother's arms, I scattered toward the only way out.

Regina's hand came up and grabbed my upper arm before I could get out of the room. "You little whore. I treated you like my own. You slept with my husband!" She let go of my arm, brought hers up, and slapped me across the face.

My father and the detective stood by and watched. My mother pulled me away from her. She was still protecting me, but the hurt and sadness in her eyes destroyed me more than being called a whore.

The last thing I heard as I ran was Regina's voice. "You are nothing more than a gold-digging whore!" Chairs slid across the concrete floor, and people pushed out of the way as I ran to the exit to escape the hell I had just endured. I refused to stop or look at anyone as I maneuvered through the police department. The doors were just yards away when I collided with a human brick wall, and I stopped dead in my tracks.

Peyton stood there in his expensive suit and glared at me. His eyes held me in place, too scared to move. There was nothing but hatred and anger pouring out of his eyes. "I warned you."

I warned you' is all he said before he stepped around me. I was no longer worthy of his time. That was all the encouragement I needed to run straight to the front doors and into obstacle number two. A man dressed in typical chauffeur attire stood next to a black limo parked right in front of the police station.

"Miss Summers, please get in the car. My employer would like to have a word with you in private." His voice was direct, leaving no room for negotiations.

"No." I wasn't about to get into another fucking limo— that is what started this shit in the first place, delivering me to the Infidelity offices and sending me straight to my demise.

The driver approached. "Get in the car—this is not a choice. I suggest you don't anger him any more than you already have."

There was no way I planned on getting into that limo. It would be probably the last thing I did. I nodded and then took a step toward the limo. I needed him to believe I would get in; then I would run. Another step and the driver grabbed my upper arm and leaned down.

"Don't," he said and shoved me into the back of the limo, and the door slammed shut. My body landed partly on the seat and partly on the floorboard.

"Miss Summers, I appreciate your agreeing to meet with me. We have a lot to discuss." The man who sat opposite of me leaned back, picked up a drink, and held his cigar to his mouth. "Drive, Peterson."

"Sir, anyplace in particular?"

"Somewhere private."

"Yes, sir."

We surged forward, and the dark window behind my head rose before his belittling began. His speech was soft, but the voice was monotone and serious.

Cold, lifeless eyes watched me while I pulled myself up into the seat. He stared at me like I was the prey, and he was the hunter. My head would soon be mounted on his wall for all to see. A trophy for future opponents not to fuck with him. "Miss Summers, I'm Alton Fitzgerald." He sipped the last of his drink and set it on the bar. "Listen closely." He took a breath. "First, this..." He pointed to the two of us. "...meeting never transpired. Right now, I have five very influential businessmen and a senator in my office."

"What does that have to do with me?"

He leaned forward, and I could smell whatever he had just drunk on his breath. "As I was saying, I am meeting with several high-power businessmen who will attest to the fact that I never left. Any attempt to report our time together and you will look like a bigger lying slut than you do now." He stopped to take a puff from his cigar. "I'll give you one guess who they will believe, and it's not you.

"Now, let's move on to the reason for this little conference." Another drag as he leaned back and blew out the smoke in my direction. "I will try to dumb it down for you to understand." He placed the cigar in a crystal ashtray. "My investigators discovered evidence that this isn't the first instance of false allegation you've made in order to force wealthy men to give you a settlement." He stopped to observe me. "Are you following, or do I need to dumb it down a little more?"

"That's a—" The words stuck in my throat as large hands wrapped around my neck and kept my lungs from inflating with oxygen. His face turned red in anger, and in that moment, I realized he reminded me of Bryce.

"You are a dumb bitch. Now shut the fuck up and listen."

The tears I held at the police station leaked from my eyes. My life flashed before me, and the only thing I saw was all the wrong decisions I made over the last year. All the mistakes I made were because of my need to prove myself.

Alton continued his speech as if his hands weren't wrapped around my neck, choking the life out of me. My hand frantically pulled at his as I gasped for air. Consciousness wavered, and he released me and shoved me back in the seat. Lightheaded and dizzy, I slouched against the leather seat as fresh air entered my body and refilled it with life.

"Miss Summers, you will recant your statement about Bryce, and in exchange, I will ensure that charges against you for filing a false police report won't be pressed. Once Bryce has been formally cleared, the documents of all the other false rape charges will disappear." He stopped to make sure he had my attention. "If you don't recant your statement, all the documents, including your signed contract with Infidelity, will be released to the papers and prove that you are a gold-digging whore. He stopped and waited for me to agree. When I didn't, he became more irritated and finished his threat. "Be assured, other men you've accused of rape have already confirmed that you liked it rough. I promise that no college, business, or man will ever look at you again."

He picked up a crystal decanter and poured himself a drink and lowered the screen behind me. "Peterson, my meeting with Miss Summers is finished."

The car stopped, and the back door opened. "Goodbye, Miss Summers, I really hope we don't have to meet again."

CHAPTER 20

The Escape
Hours later

Melissa

E xhaustion wouldn't even begin to cover how tired I was. First, Detective March interrogated and humili-ated me, calling me a whore more times than I could count. I had been slapped by my mother's best friend. Peyton dismissed me again and showed his true colors when I ran into him. Then I was shoved into a car, threatened, and now dropped off in the middle of nowhere.

The interview with March stripped away almost all of my dignity. And the little bit I had left was taken by Alton Fitzgerald. I may have been stripped of my self-respect but that is when I realized that I gained something else: the knowledge that they didn't break me.

My phone and purse were still at the police station, or

maybe my parents had gone back to the hotel by now. Either way, I had no money or way to contact anyone to pick me up, so I was stranded. I also wasn't sure I was ready to face my mother and father, and I knew I didn't want to face Regina.

Trying to contemplate the mess of my life, I walked along the sidewalk to a little park. I recognized where I was. It wasn't far from Peyton's apartment. I followed the sidewalk, walking to a bench under a tree at the back of the park. I sat and watched an occasional jogger as he or she ran through the trails.

"Miss Summers, may I sit with you?" a soft feminine voice said from behind me.

"Why?"

I didn't bother to look up as a woman came around the bench. I didn't care. I just wanted away from the damn cruel world. Hell, the sun had started to descend toward the horizon. I should have been scared that I was just approached by a stranger, but I wasn't. I didn't care anymore. No one could hurt me any more than I'd already been hurt.

I might still feel physical pain inflicted upon my body, but nothing else could faze me anymore. I was dead on the inside even though my blood still pumped through my heart. A big part of me was lost; I just hadn't realized how much until this moment.

"I'd like to help you," the woman said.

"Oh. I've had enough help for a while," I answered dismissively. "I think I'll pass."

"May I call you Melissa?"

I lifted my gaze toward the nicely dressed woman still

standing before me. "Honestly, I don't care what you call me as long as you leave."

"I believe you."

"What do you believe?" I was on the verge of tears. "That I don't care... because I don't. Or that I want you to leave? Because I do."

"May I sit with you for a few minutes?" she asked.

"Fine." I nodded to her and scooted over to the other side of the bench.

The woman sat and leaned toward me. "I know Bryce Spencer brutally beat and raped you."

My head snapped back toward the woman. "What?" I wrapped my arms around my body and leaned forward and rocked. Soft cries filled the air as her words sank into my thoughts. She was the only other person besides my mother to validate my rape, the only other person who believed me. I didn't even know this woman. But her words were something I'd needed to hear since that terrible night. I don't think I had realized how much I needed to hear the words out loud until they were spoken. It was like a weight lifted off of my shoulders.

"My name is Deloris Witt, and I'd like to help you if you're willing to help me."

As I jumped up, the validation I'd felt seconds ago vanished. "I fucking should have known. You want something from me too. I'm out of things to give. I'm empty. Why can't everyone just leave me alone?" I turned to walk away.

She stood and placed her hand on my shoulder. "Please sit. It's not what you think."

Exhaling a deep breath, I sat down and waited for the other shoe to drop. It always did.

"Melissa, I want Bryce Spencer punished, but I need your help."

"I can't come forward. Everyone already thinks I'm a gold-digging whore." I looked every which way but at her, not wanting to see the pity in her eyes before that emotion turned to disgust. I'd seen it too many times.

Mrs. Witt placed her hand on my chin and turned my face back to hers. "Listen to me. You're not a whore." Deloris spoke slowly and quietly. "Bryce is a rapist. You didn't ask to be raped."

"No, but I sold myself. So I'm no different than a whore."

I tried to turn my head away, but she kept it in place.

"Listen to me. You made a choice. It might not have been the best choice, but at the time it seemed like your only choice. We have all done things we later regret." She placed her hand over mine and clasped it. "You aren't the first person to ever work for Infidelity. You won't be the last. Earning money as a companion isn't an invitation for a man like Bryce to take what you didn't want to give. Your correlation is inaccurate. You made a decision to follow a dream, not to lose it."

I didn't know how this woman knew so much about me. "Who did you say you are?"

"I'm Deloris, and I want to help you."

"But you want me to do something. What do you need me to do?" I asked suspiciously.

"I would like you to disappear for a while," she said with a smile.

"Disappear? How? Where? Why?"

"The how is what I want to do for you. The why is not important, but the where... well, that's up to you. Think of my offer as a paid vacation to anywhere in the world. What do you say? Would you like to get away and leave all of this behind you?"

CHAPTER 21

Free at Last
Weeks Later

Melissa

I thought I'd made the decision to live my life when I signed the contract with Infidelity. I'd believed they'd offered me a chance to be free.

I was wrong.

They'd offered a chance at a dream, but it was never freedom.

I was owned, degraded, and manipulated into a life I didn't understand. Obstacle after obstacle had been thrown at me since my sixteenth birthday, and now I saw that each one had been constructed by someone whose only desire was to possess me. My dreams were insignificant in his scheme to control me. Everything that occurred had just been a means to an end.

I hadn't realized how one decision would bring me a lifetime of debt with a liability that I would never be able to repay. The price continued to grow. Each decision I'd made since that time had come with a price higher than the original commitment I'd accepted.

The decision to break my silence, which my father made for me, came with a much higher price tag than either of us expected. Once Pandora's box was opened, my life and the lives of others were forever changed and altered. Once opened, I'd acquiesced, giving statements and wanting justice for the crimes against me, but not at the cost of my reputation or life.

For once, I chose to benefit myself. I took Mrs. Witt up on her offer. I willingly walked away from my life. I had completed the first journey, now it was time to start the next.

Since the report of my disappearance, I'd learned more about the people in my life than I probably wanted to know. No one was immune from corruption and deceit. I'd watched the news about my disappearance and interviews of people who claimed they loved and missed me. These were the same individuals who'd ignored or humiliated me on a daily basis. And yet their remarks were but another abuse against me. My life had become entertainment and a way to have their fifteen minutes of fame. And then there were others, those whose comments appeared in articles and news clips, those who claimed what a beautiful person I'd been, when in reality all they were doing was protecting their lies and keeping their agendas.

Peyton was one of the biggest liars of all. Deloris let me know that my father's car accident wasn't an accident at all. It had all been a scheme masterminded by Peyton years prior. The money my father was supposed to collect from his insurance company was intentionally held up in the review process to ensure that I followed the path he wanted for me. It was one reason my parents were so desperate for money. I now understand why my dad was so determined to hold someone accountable.

Deloris also managed to find out that Peyton pulled some strings to have my scholarship request refused. The lengths Peyton went to in order to fulfill his desires may never be truly uncovered. I'm not sure if my parents even know how much he manipulated our lives. Honestly, I'm not sure if it even mattered. Melissa Summers was no more. Thanks to the help of a kind and powerful woman, Melissa had been reborn as someone else.

Through it all, Peyton has maintained his image as a respectable businessman who tried to help a young student attain her dreams and was misled—smoke and mirrors. Regina and Peyton were still together. The way I saw it, Peyton and Regina deserved each other, and one day soon karma would visit them. I'd been reassured by the woman who gave me a new life that he would be punished.

My parents were my only regret. They weren't perfect, but they did their best. The hurt I caused my mother was probably the hardest. She was a good mother, and the single person who'd stood by me. She didn't deserve the fallout or grief that my decisions caused. She lost her only daughter. She deserved better, and maybe one day she too would find peace and happiness again.

For the first time in months, I finally felt safe.

No one from my past knew my location. I'd boarded a

private plane the night I'd met Deloris. Though she'd asked me where I wanted to go, my destination was unknown. My only request for my living conditions for the next few months had been to ask to be by an ocean.

I boarded that plane as Melissa Summers and walked off in Australia as Sophia Miller. It would take time to not answer to Melissa and more time to respond to Sophia, but as Deloris explained, this was the only way I'd ever be able to live a healthy, happy life. And as she said, after my ordeal, I deserved it. She'd arranged everything: an apartment, new identity, and finances to finally be free.

The first night in Melbourne, I went to a local restaurant located right on the beach with tables under umbrellas and the bluest water just yards away. Large sailboats bobbed at a distance, and the sun beamed down onto the beautiful blue water. Waves splashed against the white sand, reminding me of the beaches where I'd been raised.

I thought Melbourne was the most peaceful place on earth until the sun lowered, and then it also became the most stunning. As the big ball of yellow slowly descended behind the horizon, pink, purple, orange, and red splayed over the blue sky as darkness took over. That night sky was filled with stars as I'd never seen. A sense of peace took over me, and I knew that no matter what happened in the future, this was now my home.

Each night since, I'd returned to the same restaurant to enjoy dinner and the sunset. Several of the waitresses and I had even become friends. Now, even though I spend my time alone, I'm never really alone.

It's the life I'd dreamt of.

Again, I was at my restaurant as the sun began its

descent, and the sunset came to life, filling the sky with all the vibrant colors. As I reached down to grab my camera and capture the beauty, someone approached me from behind.

"Miss Summers."

My heart stopped. No one here knew me by that name. Yet with only two words, I knew he wasn't from here. His accent wasn't like the locals. No one from my past should know where I was or even be able to recognize me, especially from behind. I'd cut my once-long hair into a short bob and dyed it. No longer red, it was now a deep chestnut color.

"Miss Summers." The deep American voice no longer came from behind me but was now standing directly in front of me.

Slowly, I scanned this man. He had to be in his early forties and still he was sexy as hell. Even his clothes did little to hide what was underneath. He wore dark jeans that fit his ass perfectly and a shirt that stretched across his broad shoulders. His dark, wavy hair fell onto his forehead just above his piercing green eyes that bore into me.

It was then that he knelt down so that we were eye-to-eye. His scent filled my space, and the rush to my head made me forget to be scared that he'd used my name.

"May I sit?" he asked.

I nodded my head. The smirk on his face told me that he knew of the effect he had on me.

He pulled a chair back, the new distance caused the cologne that fueled my desires to slowly dissipate, allowing me to come to my senses. "You must have me mistaken for someone else. My name is—"

"Melissa Summers," he interjected. "Remember, I already know your name? I called you Miss Summers."

This guy was starting to piss me off and scare me at the same time. "What makes you so sure that I'm this Melissa Summers?"

"Mutual friend," he said as he picked up my drink and put the straw to his mouth—his kissable mouth.

This man knew exactly what he was doing, and it had been too long since I'd had these feelings. After Bryce, I wasn't sure I ever would. I knew one thing for sure: I needed fresh air.

Standing, I pulled my drink from his hand and asked, "Do you mind?"

As I turned to walk toward the beach, he just sat there like an arrogant ass, watching me, and he laughed.

Fuck, his laugh was even sexy.

Ass, I repeated to myself.

On the shore, I was almost to the water's edge when he called my name and jogged up to me.

"Miss Summers, will you give me a minute? I'll explain who I am."

I exhaled and nodded. "Fine. Make it quick."

"My name is Jerrod. Deloris asked me to come here and check on you."

"Deloris? As in Witt? How do you know her?"

"Come," he said, offering me his hand. "Let's take a walk and I'll tell you everything."

Nodding my head, I placed my hand in his. Deloris had protected me this far. I needed to trust that she only wanted to help me now.

EPILOGUE

Melissa

The beach had become my place of solace, the fresh air and sea breeze helping to clear my head and find peace with my past. As I walked, I thought about how much my life had changed over the last year. The dream of Northwestern and the future I'd once envisioned were no longer important. Now, I lived each day like it was my last, enjoying the simpler things, such as walks along the beach and picking up seashells that had washed ashore.

Jerrod was still by my side, watching over me each day and night. He had been since the night we met. Most days he walked with me, protecting me, but on some days when he sensed that I needed space, he allowed me my alone time.

He was so different from all the other men in my past. He was kind, caring, and protective. Whenever we talked about my old life, it seemed as if he knew more than he said, but he never asked. He held me through the night-mares and kissed my forehead as a sign of affection. And yet he'd never pushed me for more than I was willing to give.

Trust was something I wasn't sure I'd ever be able to give again entirely, but I hoped that one day I would.

I still wasn't ready to have an intimate relationship, but when that time came, Jerrod would be the type of man I'd want as my forever.

Right now, I'll take one day at a time.

THE END

TO MY READERS

I would like to thank you for taking the time to read *Shattered* and follow Melissa's journey. She was created and developed in the Infidelity series by Aleatha Romig. Each character has an important role, but not every character has his or her voice heard. Melissa played a significant presence in the series; however, her story was left untold until now. *Shattered* is only a glimpse into Melissa's story and if you want to read what the future holds, I invite you to read and enjoy the Infidelity series.

ABOUT THE AUTHOR

A lifelong Florida resident, Somer Grey is married to a wonderful, understanding husband, and together they're busy raising two teenage children and catering to a demanding cat.

Somer began this journey as an avid reader who slowly became more involved and active in the indie book community. She helps run and administrate multiple Facebook pages and beta-reads for several amazing authors. She has built treasured friendships along the way.

This endeavor into writing *Shattered* wouldn't have been possible without the encouragement of family and friends, including published authors who convinced her to reach for the stars and live her dream.

www.ingramcontent.com/pod-product-compliance
Lightning Source LLC
Chambersburg PA
CBHW061154170626
46809CB00003B/1096